ON THE OTHER SIDE

ON THE OTHER SIDE

Trisha Vohra

Copyright © 2015 by Trisha Vohra.

Library of Congress Control Number:		2015915859
ISBN:	Hardcover	978-1-5144-1141-4
	Softcover	978-1-5144-1140-7
	eBook	978-1-5144-1139-1

All rights reserved. No part of this book may be reproduced or transmitted in any form or by any means, electronic or mechanical, including photocopying, recording, or by any information storage and retrieval system, without permission in writing from the copyright owner.

This is a work of fiction. Names, characters, places and incidents either are the product of the author's imagination or are used fictitiously, and any resemblance to any actual persons, living or dead, events, or locales is entirely coincidental.

Any people depicted in stock imagery provided by Thinkstock are models, and such images are being used for illustrative purposes only.
Certain stock imagery © Thinkstock.

Print information available on the last page.

Rev. date: 10/06/2015

To order additional copies of this book, contact:
Xlibris
1-888-795-4274
www.Xlibris.com
Orders@Xlibris.com
720137

*I dedicate this to my friends, family, my mom
and dad, my uncles and aunts.*

Without their support this project could not be accomplished.

Trisha

Prologue

I guess life and I were never really compatible. Why I say this? 'Cause I don't have one. I was an unwanted bundle dropped off at an orphanage far away from where I was born by a person I despise more than life in general. Worst of all, this person expected me to live on my own.

Growing up was hard. When I was little, I embraced death, letting its cold arms hug me and take me with it, but no. All it did was leave me with a kiss of torture, keeping my eyes open so wide that everything was like an open book. But things change. This is another of unwanted, underprivileged girl. As you can see, I have grown a lot due to my greater understanding of the state of life I am in right now.

Ash Kaiden Rowe.

*

Senior year. Every girl's dream, my nightmare, one more step into the real world.

Ooo, scary.

I stared into the reflection, the same blue eyes and other facial features that starkly stood on my tan skin. Ripped jeans and the same sweatshirt—that was my outfit for the first day of school last year. I took my personal relief-of-life-stress notebook off the dusty dresser and into my still surprisingly fully functional messenger bag, Betsy. Yes, I named an anatomic object. Don't judge.

The orphanage looked like a house that needed a good fixer-upper. I walked out of my room, running my hands on the chipped walls, rough on the pads of my fingers. Stepping down the east stairwell, which was right under my room, each step groaning from the abuse it has received over the years. When I reached the bottom of the steps, the sounds of clattering pots and pans filled the ground floor. Yup, the Cinderella of Upstate New York was at work, filling the mouths of kids who still needed to have their hearts filled more. The kitchen door was open, where Cook was at her best, flour on her apron and a steel bowl full of pancake mix in her hands. Walking in quietly not to disturb her when she was in her zone, I slipped onto one of the chairs that was nestled under the large dining table. She turned around to reach for something when she saw me. Her bow-shaped lips spread into a smile, revealing a straight row of teeth.

"Good morning, love." She removed her apron and put down the steel bowl, opening her arms wide for a hug. I got up without any hesitation and slipped into her warm arms. "Senior year, aren't you excited? One more year till you're out in the real world, having fun in adulthood."

I looked down at her face full of laugh lines and experience in the wild. I shook my head no. She smiled an understanding smile. Cook got what I was scared of but made sure it was kept silent. Aged dark brown eyes took one more good look at me and nodded with approval as she went back to cooking breakfast. In the whole orphanage, I was the oldest of all the children. The smell of pancakes surrounded the tiny kitchen as she flipped two on a plate for me along with a glass of her tangy orange juice. Luckily, no one else was up due to elementary and preschool starting later than the high school. I got some silverware and a checkered napkin as Cook laid my meal on the table.

"You know, when I was in high school, my friends and I had a road trip during one of our breaks. It was a lot of fun." She pulled out the chair on my opposite side and sat with her hands folded in front of her.

I put a bite of pancake and took a sip of the sweet yet sour orange juice.

"I don't know," I finally said. "There are important reasons why I would actually travel."

Ever since I was a little girl, I had always wanted to meet my parents even though I hate them. The truth is, unlike most kids in this joint, my parents are actually alive. They are hiding somewhere in my birthplace in California, where the sun always shines bright. Not always.

"You better get going. You're going to get late."

I got up, swinging good old Betsy on my shoulder. I bet you she was far more prepared for the day than I was.

"Have a good day, Ash." Cook smiled, and her laugh lines uncreased, revealing a beautiful face full of passion for the world.

*

The air was cold and dense, but the sun still shone brightly, radiating its light to every dark hole. For some reason, my stomach was full of butterflies, evil kinds with their wings flapping so fast that it created little tornadoes, which is totally strange. It's just school. I've been there a thousand times already—nothing new, nothing old.

Jackson Burrow was probably one of the oldest high schools in town, so old that your grandparents or your mom and dad attended it. Obviously not mine, but you know what I mean. I walked on the narrow paved road, dodging laughing groups or any chance of me getting knocked over and my papers go flying. Then a cute guy comes to help me. Yeah, no. It's actually not even possible. One, I have incredible reflexes especially when balancing; and two, no one would help me. Sorry to burst your bubble.

The only person who had parents is my best friend, Rose McArthur. When I spotted her, she was leaning against the brick wall, earphones in, blocking out the world's opinions but listening to her own. I began to walk to her when she ripped out her earphones and pulled me into one of her magnificently tight and deadly bear hugs.

"I missed you, Ash Ash." Her voice was muffled.

"I missed you too, Rose. How was the bite fest? I got the pictures." She let go of me and began her superlong descriptions.

I looked out to the field where groups were chattering, some laughing and others talking through their phones, though they were right in front of each other, but something else caught my eye. A silver car rolled on the black paved road until it found a parking. With much anticipation, the door swung open, and out came a boy. He slung his black backpack higher up on his shoulder as he began walking closer to the building. Conversations didn't stop, nor did anyone turn around to see who the newcomer was. When he came even closer to the front, I got to see his face. His skin was light paired with hazel eyes, all the buttons of his plaid shirt was opened, and his Converse was messily tied. Without a word, the mystery boy slipped into the building.

"Hellooo, earth to Ash!" I turned to see Rose frantically flapping her hands, attempting to get my attention. "Classes will start in three minutes. What do you have?"

I blinked once, then twice.

"Oh sorry, I have AP writing with Mr. Benson."

"Ugh, lucky butt, I have Mrs. Jonte for math, legit you can't even differentiate whether she is speaking French or trying to teach algebra." Rose has a tendency to flap her hands while she talks. It's one way she shows her emotion. The more flapping, the more annoyed she is; the less flapping, the calmer she is.

The sound of the bell rippled through the field, and everyone began to gather his or her belongings. No going back. The first day of school was ready to begin, but the question is, am I ready? The evil butterflies were back, now flapping faster than ever.

*

Mr. Benson's classroom always smelled like unopened books and pencil shavings. But I loved it. He was always the one who would mentor me on my writing, and it made me better each time. I opened the door to his classroom when I saw him at his oak desk, papers spread all over, hands on his hips. You see, Mr. Benson is a walking and talking example of a genius, always was and always will be. I slowly started approaching his desk as he looked up, and his eyes cringed with the smile upon his face.

"Hello, my dear." He pushed his glasses back a little more.

"Hi, Mr. Benson." I pulled my backpack on my shoulder higher.

"How was your summer, anything exciting?"

"Boring, as always."

He chuckled as he handed me a piece of blank paper. I began walking to my seat earning a few snickers and people whispering 'teachers pet' under their breath. Mr. Benson cleared his throat as he walked to the middle of the classroom with the crisp blank piece of paper in his hand. All the classrooms had a large white board in the front where the teacher would write. He took a magnet and placed it on top of the paper, binding it to the board. Then he turned around to the front of the classroom overlooking all the kids.

"Welcome, seniors, to AP Writing. Some of your faces are those that I know from years prior, and others yet to learn about. My name is Mr. Benson." He began walking closer to the front row of desks with a warm smile on his face. "When you walked into my classroom, I gave you something. What is it?"

Hands shot up in the air.

"Yes." He pointed at a girl with a shitload of makeup caked on her face.

"It's a piece of paper."

"Correct, but here in my class we don't call it paper. See, writing is just like art. It is beautiful, meaningful, and some are even eye catching. The only difference between writing and art is that your words are assorted colors, your pencil is your brush, and this piece of paper—" He stopped. I think it was to emphasize his words, not that he needed it but whatever floats his boat. "This piece of paper is your canvas."

The class was silent. Like anyone could top that. What I say? Raw genius. A small knock came from the door. There stood in his laid-back fashion, the mystery boy. Benson tuned around and nodded at him before he began talking again.

"Your assignment is to paint you canvas with whatever and however you want."

He turned once more and began engaging a conversation with him. I let the world do what it wanted, but all I wanted to do was paint my canvas. Picking up my pencil, I began writing the first thing that came to mind. Mystery boy.

"Ash, please come here, dear." Mr. Benson popped his head into the classroom

The train of thought that I was going to transfer onto my canvas now had to wait. Yay. I put the pencil down and walked to the door, stepping out into the quiet and dead hallway. That's where Mr. Benson stood, and behind him, my newly feared mystery boy. I wanted to crawl into a hole and stay there for forever.

"Ash, my dear, come closer." I paddled over, and I swore when I looked at mystery boy, his lips went up a notch. "This is Jake Watterson, the new student that will be attending this school and our AP writing class, and out of all the student . . ." Out of all the student, what? "I have chosen you to mentor him."

For a moment, happiness jolted to each nerve in my body, then it subsided. Jake and his sharp hazel eyes were probably going to get taken by someone better than me. And that was the end of it. I didn't need another heartbreak, after all I have had enough. I nodded politely understanding that how he would do was up to me. Might as well call me Ms. Ash, here to help. Ha. No.

"I will let you guys get acquainted with each other while I go answer some questions inside the class." He curtly nodded and went back inside.

Will I ever going to be able to finish my class work? Nope. I turned around to see Jake smiling at me. It was like eternity till he spoke. Jeez that was mushy yuck.

'What's your name, Blue Eyes?" His voice was like velvet.

"Ash." I debated whether to use my full name or not. "Ash Kaiden Rowe." My voice came out scratchy.

"So you're my mentor, huh? Don't worry I'll be a good student." He gave a charming smile, though the string of words that came out of his mouth were majorly perverted. Was he high? Why the hell was he flirting with me?

"Okay, well, I think we should get back inside." Before he could reply, I was walking into the classroom.

Jake followed me in as Mr. Benson was lecturing about the quality of the work that he would grade. The rest of the class was kind of a blur. We wrote some and talked some.

All I could think of were those playful dancing hazel eyes.

*

During lunch, Rose and I hung out by the outcast wall as we call it.

"So how was writing? Heard there was a new student." She took a bite out of her club and sipped her iced tea out of those useless bendy straw things.

"Yeah, and I was assigned to be his mentor."

"Wow. I am surprised that Alex and her crew didn't stick a fork up your butt yet"

Alex, being one of the obnoxious girl version of a player. She and her friends had like a dib system on any guy that would walk through the crusty school doors.

"I guess she used the leftover brain cells, that she surprisingly had, to sum up that she was anyway going to get him and that he's probably going to become a jock."

She laughed.

"Well, you never know, tables turn, things change." She took a bite of her sandwich again.

"Has my mom ever come back for me?"

"No." She took her time saying that one tiny word as if it was going to come out at me and eat my face off, then stab me for good measure. But surprisingly, it didn't.

"Then tables turning is just a metaphor that means nothing and proves nothing."

Rose said nothing, because it was true, and nothing was going to change my mind.

*

The day went by with ease. I gathered my books, stuffing them into my bag fast, so that the swarms of kids trying to catch their bus home won't swallow me up. I walked into the hallway going to the left wing where the nearest exit door stood patiently waiting. I felt a small touch on my shoulder and immediately turned around assuming self-defense posture. Just kidding, I gave the shoulder tapper the death glare. The shoulder tapper was Jake, his signature crooked smile plastered on his face.

"What are you up to, Blue Eyes?" His smile grew when I rolled my eyes.

"Well, clearly I am trying to get out of here fast." I turned around to walk away from him and his too-handsome-for-you face, just for him to follow me out.

"Are you walking?" He swung his car keys around his pointer finger.

"Yep." I walked up the stairs to the sidewalk leading to my way home.

"Lemme give you a lift." He leaned against the reddish brown brick wall.

"No, I'm good." I started walking again.

"Aw come on, why not?"

He asked for it, and it was the perfect time to tell him. I walked back to him and looked up to the wall.

"You see that slot with the missing brick?" He walked closer to me and turned around facing the wall once again.

"Yes, I think so." He ran his fingers through his hair.

"The black slot represents me, people like me. We are different, unwanted, otherwise known as the outcasts." I pointed to the newly applied flawless bricks. "Those bricks are the ones who fit in. You might not know what I am saying but, you're new, you have a big chance to fit into that crowd, be the star."

He turned to look at me.

"What if I said I cared less about being the star? What if I didn't need to be popular or cool?"

I stood there speechless, utterly confused on what just happened.

"Then you're stupid" I felt my lip tilt up the tiniest notch.

"So is that a yes for me driving you home?" His lazy smile again.

I laughed wholeheartedly as he led his way to the shiny silver car. And as the gentlemen that he was, he opened the door for me, bowing like a butler. Once again I rolled my eyes but smiled.

"Okay, where do you live?" He slid the key in the ignition slot and turned it until I heard the roar of the engine "That totally did not sound creepy."

"Pretty close from here. Just make a left there and go straight on the road." He did exactly what I asked until we were right in front of the orphanage. Luckily, it looked like a house 'cause I was most definitely not ready to tell him.

"See? It wasn't that bad," he said, playfully. "Hey, before you go, can I have your number just so that if I have any questions on homework, I can ask it to you?"

I nodded as I pulled out my phone, and we exchanged numbers.

"Thanks for the lift." I opened the car door and pulled my backpack on my shoulder. As I softly shut the door, he nodded.

"Anytime, Blue Eyes."

I felt a smile creep on my face as I looked down at the newly saved contact. But wait, we were only in one class together, which was Mr. Benson's class, and he never assigns homework on the first day of school.

Dammit.

I shut the door behind me, removing my shoes.

"How was school?" I heard Cook call out from the kitchen.

"It was . . . great."

Good morning, blue eyes ☺

My phone was the one to wake me up at about six forty-five doing the pee pee dance on my nightstand.

You woke me up, Jake :(

I combed out my hair and pulled it into a braid by the time he responded.

I believe it's pronounced, wake-up text.

I giggled at his response.

What do you want?

Lol did you sleep well, blue eyes?

Not sure yet, since you woke me up halfway. Hbu?

Not too good. I had this question I needed to ask you that kept me up all night.

Okay what is it?

Would you like to go to the pancake house for dinner with me?

What? Did he just ask me out?

What's today?

It's Friday, blue eyes, I would never ask you to go out with me on a weekday, I have homework to do ☺.

I thought about it. If I go, I will probably get my heart broken, if I don't go, I will jeopardize our friendship. Just do it.

Yes I'll go.

Great. Pick you up at 6, blue eyes.

Okay igtg to school.

Look outside.

I did. His silver car was parked, and he was standing there. I never ran down the stairs that fast in my life.

"Woah, slow down!" Cook stood at the bottom of the steps with a wooden spoon in her hand. "Who is outside, Ash?"

"A friend. Who may be a male."

And once I said that, Cook pulled me into a gigantic hug grinning like a Cheshire cat.

"You better go. He's waiting, and it's not too warm out there." She waved me off as she went back into the kitchen.

My breath came out as white smoke, and my shoes crunched onto the frosted grass. Jake stood with a smile on his face, looking like a model asked for his number. Honestly, I wouldn't be surprised if that actually happened.

"Malady, your chariot awaits." He still needed to work on that accent, but it was hilarious anyway. "Next stop . . ." He walked around that car as I buckled in. "To school."

We talked some, then laughed some till we got in the parking lot. Rose stood with confusion written on her face. I walked to her and whispered in her ear.

"He asked me out, and I said yes. Be nice please." She looked at me, eyes wide. I could have sworn that they were going to fall out of her socket and roll all the way to Mexico. "Oh my god, congratulations!"

*

Mr. Benson tapped the wooden gavel on the podium in front of the class, easily winning our attention.

"Today, I am going to be lecturing you on feelings and emotions, which I am well aware that you all have a lot of knowledge on due to your hormones being on fleek. When you're writing, the strongest parts are your negative and positive emotions due to the experiences you may have when you put these kinds of emotions in a story. It makes it worthwhile to read and write it. Today, I want you to write something that means a lot to you using these two emotions." He walked back to our desk allowing us to write out our emotions.

I put my pencil on my paper and began writing.

*

Six o'clock was coming a lot faster than expected. I closed my writing book where I was completing Mr. Benson's assignment and took a good look at the mirror. I did what I usually do to my hair, let it go into a braid. I put on some denim jeans and a sweater that Cook got for my birthday. Walking into the bathroom, I brushed my teeth for the fifth time. The sound of the doorbell echoed throughout the orphanage.

Shit.

I flew down the stairs like gravity was nothing to me. Surprisingly, no one was by the door. Most of the younger kids would go there to see if someone said the wrong address for pizza. But no one was there. I opened the door as I slipped on the converse to see Jake standing wearing a leather jacket, jeans, and a beanie. Damn.

"Hello, Blue Eyes, ready to have an awesome breakfast for dinner?" He took my arm and curled it under his own. The shiny silver car was standing proudly in front.

"Yeah, I guess. Where are we going again?" I fumbled around with my words a bit, hoping he wouldn't be able to tell.

"The one and only pancake house." He smiled as he held the door out for me.

*

The pancake house smelled like maple syrup and coffee. The place was almost empty except for a couple of booths occupied by other teens.

"For how many?" A lady asked.

"Two please," answered Jake. His smile lit his facial features.

The lady slipped out two menus and proceeded straight across the diner and seated us at one of the booths. Once we had our menus, she left us to think. Jake's green eyes scanned the old menu, full of coffee stains and circles.

"I am going to get the pancakes." He put down his menu and looked at me

"I'll get the waffles." I mimicked his position.

"Ash Kaiden Rowe, what a beautiful name, yet I don't know anything about you." He leaned back, examining my face as if it were art, the sparkle in his eyes never failing.

"Well, I am not really that fascinating."

"I can most definitely disagree with that."

Thankfully, the waitress came to take our orders.

"Now tell me about yourself." Darn it, he didn't forget. *Oh well, grow up and tell him*, I thought.

"Well, I am an orphan. The house that you always come to pick me up from is the orphanage. I was shipped from California, my birthplace, like I was unwanted cargo. I grew up alone with me being my own backbone. At a young age, I knew the harsh reality of loneliness and pain." I looked into his green eyes. "I always hated my mom, and though that hatred was supported with huge reasons, I wanted to meet her. Who is she, who was I, who am I. Through someone, I found out my biological birth father left my mom, so I guess I got used to that."

I stopped for a moment, then went on.

"Life went on without a cause. I thought that maybe, just maybe, she would come back for me, but they never did. From a young age, I was different. I never spoke to people, but when I did I was harsh. I never cared what people thought of me. Writing was the only place where I allowed myself to shed a single tear, to show any emotion. I found out that I was different from the other kids in the orphanage. Their parents are actually dead, but mine are not. They are together, somewhere in my birthplace, hiding. I have known Rose since forever. She was the only who got me and had parents. So we hung out, talked. And now here we are, senior year, having no beginning or an ending, just swinging from the middle without a destination."

I looked at him from my hooded lashes.

*

"After you, Blue Eyes." Jake held the door open for me as we exited the diner.

"Thanks for everything." I stopped and looked up to him. "I know you said that you took me out today, but do you really want to date someone like me? Someone that is broken?"

He turned around and looked at me, his usual joking around and playfulness nature had checked out.

"All your life, you lived through shit. On top of that, you know your mom is alive, and she just left you. Which adds on top of that shit, making it a double pile of shit. And you asked me if I was sure to date the most beautiful and amazing girl I have ever met."

Well, when he said it like that.

"Really?"

"Yes, Blue Eyes, really?"

I just stared at him. Damn, I was so deep.

*

(Two months and countless dates later)

Light streamed through the blinds, sufficiently waking me up from a peaceful oblivion. I began to get up, making my way to the bathroom. What did Jake ever see in me? My complexion was just so plain. A knock came from my door, and Cook peeked her head in.

"Honey, you got some company." She walked in, softly shutting the door behind her.

"Who is it?" I began braiding my hair.

"It's your male friend." Cook began to chuckle, sitting on the corner of the bed. "Ash, he seems like a nice boy."

I stared at my reflection in my mirror, nodding back to her. She got up, walking toward me, putting her hands on my arms.

"Go." Her hands moved up and down, warming up my arms. "He is waiting."

I nodded again, walking outside of my room and down the staircase. Jake stood by the door way, hand in his pocket, wearing a plaid shirt and a beanie, a dimple pitting his cheek as he smiled.

"Morning, Blue Eyes." He held his arms out in a waiting-for-you-to-hug-me motion.

I came closer and took his hand, giving it a good shake.

"It's all good. One day you will realize that awesome power of my hugs."

"Yeah, and that day wouldn't be today." I began to make my way to the kitchen, picking up the plate of breakfast that Cook had made for me, Jake trailing close behind.

"Ouch, Blue Eyes, you wound me." I rolled my eyes and began shoving the food into my mouth. "Anyhow, wanna come over?"

"How could I decline?" I smiled, finishing the last bits of my breakfast.

I waved at Cook, letting her know I was going out, then I took my coat, and we made our way toward the car.

*

Jake and I talked and walked around his part of the neighborhood. We both went quite for a few minutes. He stared hard at something in the distance.

"Come on, I . . ." He unlocked a shed in his backyard. "Wanna show you something."

Behind the doors of shed was a little art studio decked out with tons of painted canvases. Some were on the tables, others were on the ground, and one painting was on an easel. It was a painting of a girl. It looked completed to my eyes.

"This one is for you." He came around me, plucking the canvas off the easel. "It's supposed to be a painting of you bu—"

"Shut up." I took the canvas. "Thanks, it's beautiful."

"Brace yourself, this is going to be super cheesy," clearing his throat. "You are more beautiful."

I laughed, and when I laughed I just couldn't stop.

"I was expecting you to go all googly eyes, maybe a hug."

That made me laugh harder.

"One more thing." I looked up at him trying to keep the laugh that was bubbling its way up my throat back. "I was thinking, since you aren't doing anything during break—"

"What makes you think that I am not doing anything over break?" I said stuffing the painting into Betsy.

All I got was the look.

"Okay, okay, point to you!"

"Well, I was thinking. Do you want to go to California to find your mom? I haven't worked anything out yet. It was just an idea." He rubbed his hand on the back of his neck.

What the what now?

"B-bu-but the money and permission and Mother . . . and California?"

He smiled a dazzling smile. "I'll pay everything. Again I haven't worked anything out yet, for permission we are going got have to finger something out."

I think I know a way. I took Jake's hand and ran all the way to his car.

*

"Hello I am Ramona, better known as Cook to the kids." We were in the kitchen as Cook poured three cups of steaming cup of coffee.

"Hi, I am Jake, Ash's boyfriend."

I couldn't help the blush that snuck on my cheeks from his declaration.

"Nice to meet you." Cook beamed her smile, fitting perfectly on her face. "So you guys needed something. What is it?"

"Well, you see," I started just to get cut off by Jake, luckily.

"Ash and I were discussing that she want to go to meet her parents in California during winter break, and I would like to go with her, so we needed permission."

Her eyes lit up, trying to take that in.

"Okay, so you guys are asking me to give you permission to go to California to search for Ash's parents. Look, I honestly think it's an excellent idea. But, Ash," she turned to me, a sweet smile on her face, "the question to ask is that if you are ready to this, asking the headmaster is not a big problem."

I looked into her soft hazel eyes perfectly describing her personality.

"I'm ready. I want to go. This is something that is important, and I am not going to miss it like how I did to most of them."

"Okay, officially you are busy during break." She smiled and drained the rest of her coffee down.

*

Blue eyes, are u busy today?

It was Saturday afternoon, and I was lying on my bed, just writing some more of Mr. Benson's assignment. I picked up the phone and began writing a response back to him.

Me: No just writing Mr. Benson's assignment.
Bae: I have some news for the trip. Can I come over?
Me: Yeah, sure, come over.
Bae: Okay, I'll be there in ten.

Thoughts flew into my head. For the first time, I wanted this so bad that I was willing to do anything for it, anything at all. I walked down each and every step oh so carefully. I grew up here, but this wasn't where I was born. Every step I took was like every choice I made. I can never erase them, but they were there for a significant meaning. And this time, it's going to be different. I will not back down. This time I will plant my footstep so that no one can take it off. Ever. When I was at the bottom of the steps, Jake and Cook were talking. But Cook had the smallest smile on her face.

"Hey, Ash." Jake was wearing his plaid shirt with jeans. "So about the trip, I have something for you."

He flipped the fabric and closed his brown rustic satchel up, taking out two pieces of paper. Examining the papers, he handed me one of them. I read the top line. It was the ticket to go to California. The letters blurred in my vision.

"The headmaster said yes, and your passport is ready." This time, it was Cook's voice.

I put the precious piece of paper down on the antique table and jumped onto Jake. He caught me with ease but stumbled back a little. My shoulders shook and my chest tightened. I hated crying, I hated showing weakness, but I couldn't stop now. All the pain I felt was going to finally be supported by a reason, two reasons actually. I cried because I had to, I needed to let it out.

"It's okay, Blue Eyes, everything is going to be okay, I promise." I felt him sit. I was still in his lap as he drew soft shapes on my back. "Don't worry, we'll find them, just let it out, it will be okay, and if not, I will make it okay."

I stopped shuddering, no tear came out, but all I knew was that Jake had held on to me for that long period, never letting go. I looked up at his face.

"You better, Blue Eyes?"

I nodded.

*

I plopped the suitcase that Cook lend me. Rose sat on the bed and inspected every detail of it. After the deep analysis, she finally commented, "Well, it's a suitcase."

"Yeah, I know, but what would I pack for California. I have no dresses and mostly, I just own jeans and sweatshirts." Clothes frustrated me. Just looking at them made me feel like I was on *Fashion Police*.

"I think that's why I am here, to help my little fashion stresser." She giggled as she took my hand and led me to the kitchen. "If I don't say so myself, you're awesome at hiding stuff!"

She did a little fan-girl clap and spin. Cook opened one of the cupboards taking out some shopping bags, each had different colors and logos. Once again, she thanked Cook swooped the bags, and pulled me back to my room.

"Okay, so there are some dresses for fancier occasions, and others are top and shorts and stuff like that. Oh my god, you're going to look gorg!"

I looked at my best friend's face, the excitement she had for getting me clothes.

"Thank you so much, Rose." She began waving me off.

"Less slackin', more packin'!"

*

I took one more good look at the orphanage. It was nine in the morning, and a large black car with a driver and Jake was parked in front.

"Ready to go, Blue Eyes?" He threw an arm over my shoulder, green eyes searching my face.

Cook came closer to me and gave me hug. She took my hand and wrapped it around a small box.

"This little box is a present from me to remind you that we are always here for you." Tears rolled down her cheek as she gave me a watery smile. She ran her hands up and down my arms.

"Don't worry I will never forget you."

She nodded and followed me to the car. I hopped in, feeling the soft thud of the door. The angry butterflies were back shooting out tornadoes like darts hitting a target. I looked back at the orphanage, but it was nothing but a dot.

*

The airport reminded me of high school, everyone was different and they all have a different destination. I stayed close to Jake without going inside of him. Pretty sure he got claustrophobic at some point, but he was just going to have to suck it up. We approached a counter to check in our luggage. I watched closely as Jake pulled the bags onto the conveyor belt leading into a flapped screen.

"Taking notes over there, Blue Eyes?" He took my hand as he rolled the small carry-on suitcase. "Okay, next stop is the security check-in."

We went down the escalator toward a huge ass line of people. I began advancing over when I felt a small tug on my elbow.

"Oh no, we aren't going on that line. See, that's economy class," he said, pointing toward a sign overhead the crowd. "We are traveling business class like the cool people."

I chuckled.

*

An hour of trying to find our terminal is a lot more excruciatingly done than said. I plopped on the chair that looked pretty beat up. My fingers wrapped around the metal handle of the chair. Hmm, that's interesting, there was something squishy. I looked under the handle to find my finger deep into a wedge of gum someone so graciously left for me. Jake plunged into the chair next to me, throwing an arm over my shoulder. I looked out at the people in the airport. A lady in a business suit scurried away as she yapped on the phone about not doing it right. I looked up at Jake who was asleep, which would probably be better than accidentally eavesdropping in other people's conversations, making it an awkward situation for yourself. I cuddled closer attempting to enclose myself into Jake's warmth. I slowly drifted into my dreams of California and my mom.

*

"Blue Eyes, wake up, time to go. Don't make me kiss you." My eyes sprang open.

Jake was above me, hands on my shoulders. I heard the soft muffle of our flight being called. He took my hand and pulled me up, allowing me to walk in front of him.

"Boarding pass please." A lady with super white teeth and red lipstick on her perky lip said, jutting out her hands.

"Okay, one more stop to Cali baby." Jake began putting our bags on the top compartment as I slid into the blue leather chair.

The sun was beginning to set, casting rays of red and yellow throughout the sky. It was honestly beautiful. I leaned back onto my chair, paying extra attention to the safety directions that was thrown to me by a lady who sounded like she might want to hibernate for the remainder of her life. The lady walked away taking her seat as the plane began to move.

"Ready, Blue Eyes?"

I nodded. The plane began accumulating speed faster and faster and faster. I squeezed my eyes not daring to open them as we were airborne.

*

I think it was my fiftieth time peeing. Carefully sliding into my seat, careful not to wake Jake up, I slid the window up. It was dark but the stars were twinkling. Below was just the ocean, dark blue and waves crashing.

"What would you like to drink?" The air hostess pointed at me.

"Um . . . I'll just take two waters for both of us."

She smiled and handed me two water bottles. I leaned back again right before I drifted. The last thing I saw was those two people out of a million.

*

"Attention, passengers, we will now be landing. Have extreme caution when opening overhead compartments due to luggage shifting throughout the flight. Thank you, and I hope you enjoy your stay in California."

My eyes opened to see Jake smiling like a kid on Christmas. He pulled me by the arms and hugged me super tight. I laughed.

"We survived the flight, Blue Eyes!"
"Hey, I wasn't that bad."
"Sure you weren't, Blue Eyes." He goaded.

*

Welcome to California.

Wow we are here, just two people in a big city on a mission. Palm trees were everywhere, and the sun was shining and heat radiated everywhere. I turned around to see Jake smiling at me.

"Liking the scenery?" I asked waiting for his smartass reply.

"Oh, of course." He winked.

"So what's the plan?" I turned around to look at his face fully.

"Well, we are going to stay at a hotel, and of course since we are in beautiful California, we will go around as well as look for your parents." He smiled, satisfied with his plan.

The car drove for at least an hour until it sopped at hotel. People were coming and going from the place, trolleys full of luggage rolling by, and kids were running. Everything was happy. Jake took my hand.

"Your majesty, the castle awaits." He winked.

The stairs were marbled, and the hotel looked a little old, but it was perfect. He was perfect. There was a beautiful oak desk, and behind it was a smiling man. He looked a bit creepy 'cause he didn't stop smiling but whatever. Jake began talking to him in his laid-back manner, while I walked around the lobby. There was a huge center seating that reminded me of cotton candy, a light pink color with a shimmery tint. I walked across to the big oak door and peeped out of the married windows. Palm trees were scattered and an inground, wait no, two inground pools were stationed.

"Okay, well, the kind man over there said that the elevator was south of the reception desk." Jake stood, clutching brochures and keys. "Do you by any chance have a compass?"

I rolled my eyes and turned around following the arrow leading to the now closing elevator. Oh shit. Jake bolted, dragging me along. There was an elderly couple already inside the transporting box. The man began jabbing at buttons making it stop, and the doors pried open. Jake began laughing and I joined in. He pulled me in a gigantic hug. I turned around to see the couple smiling at us. The elevator ascended a couple of floors until it took a full stop.

"Have a good day." The lady said smiling. Do I have a grandma as nice as her?

*

Room 301.

The halls were nice, a velvety carpet thing and base walls with tons of gold swirls.

"Okie-dokie, this is your room." He slipped the key into an electric thingamajiggy that was on the front of the door.

There was a small click allowing us to access the room. There was a bed, TV, vanity closet, and other utilities. It was perfect. I walked closer to the window. The view was beautiful, overlooking the city and palm trees right below us.

"It's going to look awesome when everything is lit up at night. I am in the room right next to you if you ever get lonely." He pointed at a door on the wall with a similar electronic thing that was on the front door. "Simply slip this key in there, and voila, you are not lonely anymore, not that you will be. Luggage will come shortly. Anything else, Blue Eyes?"

I ran over and gave him a hug. He stiffened but then wrapped his arms around me drawing me closer. For the first time, I felt like I wasn't the runner in a race known as life, but the winner. The wall that was placed in front of me was slowly lifting revealing small sparks of light.

*

My suitcase was basically empty when I put the last article of clothing in the closet. At the very bottom of the suitcase was an orangey large folder. I don't remember putting that in there. My heart skipped a beat, maybe two, okay four, don't judge. I picked up the envelope. The exterior was smooth, plain.

"What'cha up to, Blue Eyes?"

Now my heart jumped like fifty beats.

"Well, I was unpacking and"—I turned around to look at him—"I found this." I waved the envelope around. He walked over shutting the door that joined our rooms.

"Hmm, well, we can't do anything unless we look inside, so let's look inside." He waved me toward the couch.

I walked over with the envelope still clutched in my hands. I laid the envelope harmlessly on my lap.

"So you gonna open it or stare at it? I am pretty sure envelopes don't have the ability eat you." I narrowed my eyes at him. He mimicked my posture then laughed when I swatted him.

My thumb slipped under the flap, successfully hearing a tear unsealing it. Inside were crisp pieces of paper, which looked like they were kept in good condition. One of the papers was hand written, the other was a typed document. The words *birth certificate* was printed on the top. Then in smaller print was my name, Ash Kaiden Rowe. Jake took the handwritten note and started reading.

"Dear, Ash, you're doing something so very near and dear in your heart. Finding one person out of a thousand and putting the last pieces of your puzzles together is hard. But throughout, your life I have been there to help. The other piece of paper is a document, your birth certificate, that may help through this journey. Remember no matter what, everyone deserves a chance to live and learn from their mistakes. Love to you and Jake, Cook." Jake looked up at me and smiled. I mean smiled like his dreams came true before his big green eyes.

I looked at him.

"I am guessing this is definitely a good thing?" I fidgeted with the certificate.

"Yes, it is, Blue Eyes, because this is a start. We can research about this hospital and then look at your other birth records. And bam, possibly we can find a name and address or a number."

Now I smiled; that crafty Cook always got a trick or two up her sleeves.

"We can start researching tonight after I take a shower and get changed." I looked at the time: 4:00 p.m.

"Yeah sure, I have my laptop."

Pure excitement and terror flustered through me.

Jake's fingers flew across the keys of his MacBook Pro.

"Okay, well, the birth certificate says that the hospital's name is Cronstanious Hospital."

"Okay." He typed in the name and clicked the first result. "Found it. It has a maternity ward, which is our destination."

"So that's were my documents would be."

"But the question is if they allow you to look at the documents." He rubbed his hand on his plaid pajama pants.

"Well, I do have the birth certificate which is a legal document, and it has my name on it, so technically I should have the right to look at them."

He looked at me.

"That's true. We just have to hope that this applies in the situation, if not, it's going to get a lot harder than expected."

I nodded.

"All right." His normal playful smile inched back on his face. "Well, we are still on vacation, so I have an idea."

"Okay, shoot." I raised my eyebrows waiting for an outrageous remark to fly from his mouth.

"There is a mountain trail, and I've heard from a friend that it has a brilliant view of the city."

I looked out the window.

"Better than that window as well as a lot more realistic. What do you say, Blue Eyes?"

Live life, and being boxed up doesn't count.

"Sure, why not."

*

The air was warmish cold when we stepped out of the excruciatingly packed lobby and the almost-vacant sidewalk.

"Ready to be scarred for life in a good way of course?" He waved his arms toward the trail sign.

"I don't think scars are supposed to be classified in a good way." I smiled at him.

Jake began to laugh. I could see his white teeth even though the darkness was beginning to set in. He cleared his throat.

"I beg to differ, Ms. Rowe." His attempt at a British accent was quite refreshing. "There is always a bad in good and a good in bad."

There is always a bad in good and a good in bad. The words replayed in my mind like a scratched CD. I felt his eyes on me.

"I was thinking, nobody knows the true definition of life. Yet each and every metaphor that was ever made describes it"—I kicked a rock—"piece by piece."

"I'm pretty sure the point of life was to be harder than Sudoku."

I laughed bumping shoulders with him. There were trees everywhere, some higher than the others. We talked about the most random things. I would've been embarrassed to go out with a boy, to go this far, but I wasn't. I felt normal, like I've done this before. Is this what love is? Oh crap.

"Look, that's our destination."

The sidewalk led us to a railed clearing. I walked closer, Jake tagging behind me. I hadn't yet realized how high we were; below us was a bustling city. Neon lights danced on buildings, everything was lit up, cars beeping. It was full of life. I plopped down beside Jake who was staring at me instead of the scenery.

"So tell me about you." He leaned back, placing his arms behind him.

"Well, you know basically everything—"

"I only know about the dilemma with your parents which leads us in the beautiful city of California." He looked at me.

"Well, that leads to school. I felt awkward, out of place, when I was in preschool. We had little concerts where parents would come to watch. Of course all the other kids have parents leading them to come, and me always performing for myself. I knew I was different 'cause while other girls would play with Barbie's and have fun with dressing up, I would go home and write. I was made fun of because I was different, and I always thought different was bad. I tried making friends, I truly did, but some things just don't work out. So I grew up different, and I learned not to care. But sometimes words just come back to slap me on the face." I just decided to look forward at the view, honestly I felt kind of stockerish.

He didn't say anything for like ten minutes. I got kind of scared thinking I did something wrong.

"You see all the buildings?"

"Yes."

"All the buildings resemble people. They all have different structures, styles, colors. But at the end, they all have the same purpose, to hold something very important. Being different is just another word for excellence." He turned to me. "Never put yourself down because you're different."

I didn't know how to reply to that. Now, I definitely saw how he's Mr. Benson's nephew.

"Thank you." I looked at him through the thin layer of shine in my eyes.

"Don't thank me for the truth, Blue Eyes."

He put his arm around my shoulder, and I leaned in closer, lying my head on his chest. We watched as jets flew overhead, and the light danced through the city right below us.

*

"Rise and shine, Blue Eyes. We have a big day today!"

I tossed around in the puffy hotel blanket to see Jake walking in casually. I raised my eyebrows in question.

"I shouldn't have to knock if I have key." He flapped the card in the air with a sly grin. "Okay, I called down for breakfast, and then we will be going to the hospital."

I yawned, throwing the sheets off me.

"Okay, well, I am going to take a shower, so . . ." My words drifted off, hoping he got my message.

"No problem, I'll stay out here." He plopped onto the couch. "Don't worry I'll try extra hard not to peek." He winked, which made my already pink face turn to flaming red.

I scurried to the closet taking out the simplest clothes that Rose got and ran into the bathroom with a laugh, Jake still on the couch.

*

The ends of my hair ticked my cheek as I threw my dirty pajamas in the knitted bamboo hamper. The smell of coffee and toast hit my nose like a sucker punch in the gut. Jake was lying on the bed; a tray of fresh untouched food was right next to his hip.

"Ah, there you are, wonder women."

'What up T-shirt reference'

"So what's the plan?" I took a swing of the coffee and a crunch of the perfectly toasted toast.

"Well, thanks to Cook, we have a start. I found out the way to the hospital and lucky for us, it is actually in a fair amount of walking distance, so while going all James Bond, we can also be undercover tourists." I couldn't deny the little laugh that burst out of me with that analogy.

*

Different from yesterday, the streets were full of life. People catching busses, tourists were pretty obvious taking selfies everywhere.

"Brown Street is that way." Jake's phone had a map installed so we were just following that.

There were little stands everywhere, people selling little magnets and tours of the Valley Wine tasting some guy handed.

What do you got there, Blue Eyes?" He looked at the pamphlet.

"It says it's about a jail adventure, not sure if it's good for couples."

"Oh, it has a bouncy house." He pointed at the picture of some kids in an inflatable bouncy house.

We walked some more till we heard an ambulance roar and turned in the corner. So I'm guessing we were there. The hospital was a lot more crowded than the hotel, people from all ages walking in and out. A woman with a stomach, looking like she had way too much thanksgiving dinner, rolled past us on a stretcher, groaning.

"Excuse me, ma'am." Jake cleared his throat, politeness and pure sophistication mended its way into his voice. "Were is the maternity ward?"

The lady looked up from that fascinating computer, an eyebrow shot up. Yep I am guessing she was as confused as I was.

"Go through the right lane. That should take you to a separate building." She stared at us.

"Thank you."

We began walking through a hall of exiting patients. It was surrounded by glass. Honestly it was pretty nice for a hospital. We approached a door that led us out of the building we were just in and into a new one. The walls were painted a soft pastel blue with light pink stripes. Across the room was a glass wall, and behind it were tons of tiny babies in small plastic container like things. On the front was a piece of paper protected in a plastic holder, some of them had pink hats others with blue. Why so stereotypical?

Focus on the task at hand.

Jake took my hand and looked at me, nodded at the small sliding window-like thing with a small desk jutting out, spread with pamphlets. The blonde behind the desk was yelling for a file when she turned around, smiling staring at Jake like he was an angel.

"How may I help you two?" If she looked at Jake one more time, I was about to pull out a handful of her blonde hair.

"Um."

The spark in her eyes disappeared when she looked at me.

"Well, I need to look at a file."

She pursed her lips and then dialed a number on the doctor phone. I heard some mumbling and then she put the phone down.

"Okay, so there is a separate room where all the files are stored. I'll give you the directions. The girl who works with the files will help you from there. Just go through that door and stop at room A54. 'Kay?" The whole time she was talking to Jake, I rolled my eyes.

"Thank you." He smiled back. Now I was going to pull out some teeth from Jake's mouth.

I began walking, Jake catching up.

"You jealous, Blue Eyes?" His voice blowing on my ear. I whacked him in his stomach, which basically did nothing.

I stopped at the door and looked at the number again 'cause it would be kind of embarrassing to walk in a patient's room counting that we were in the maternity ward. The door was creaky and the knob was kind of sticky. Thank god there was hand sanitizer everywhere. Papers and manila folders were scattered, piled sky high.

Well, this was going to take a while.

Small rustling noises came from the back of the room where a girl about our age came out. At least she didn't go all goo-goo eyes on Jake.

"So are you looking for a file?" She looked at Jake. "You don't look like Channing Tatum."

So that's what blondie was saying. Jake shrugged.

"Yeah, we are looking for a file." I looked around again.

"Okay." She began walking toward the desk. "The hospital has mandatories, like questioning requirements."

She took out a piece of paper and a stapler.

"Do you have any official paper aka birth certificate?" Jake shuffled through his backpack and took out the paper. "Hmm, that's strange, the slot where your birth giver should be is blank."

There was supposed to be a name there?

"Well," I said, "yes, we have the official birth certificate, and I am trying to find my mother."

She scribbled that down on the paper.

"Well, you answered the second question, reasoning of looking at file, so I guess we should start looking."

*

I never believed in the saying "A baby is born every minute," but now I do. If I see paper again, it was going to be too soon, and the worst part was that if I was already exhausted, then that means Jake was too. But he looked fine actually, enjoying himself, laughing at the names people decide for their kids.

"Ash, I think I found it." The girl now known as Lilly waved the file like it was a flag.

I looked at her then the file. She stuck it out and I slowly took it. The desk was the only place where there wasn't any paper in sight, the two tagged along both peering over my shoulder, which did feel a bit awkward. There were only a couple papers, and like my birth certificate they all had no name. Not one.

"Hey wait, let me see that for a sec." Lilly took the first paper full of information. "Look, up here is an insurance number. If this person used this card number, we can possibly check if there is an address or a name. But since it looks like they didn't want you to know anything about them, there might have just been either or. Then again it's honestly worth a try."

I nodded. It's our best bet, the only bet. She began typing and then calling. Anticipation was building. I started humming "Lego House" by Ed Sheeran 'cause it was a make-or-break moment, totally appropriate for this moment. Jake sauntered over and threw his arm on my shoulder. We waited, all we did was wait. All I ever did was wait. Lilly began scribbling something down. She put the phone down and smiled.

"Well, we're in business. They said there was a blockage. Around the year you were born, all information about the insurance cardholder was blocked off. But not all access. Of where the payment had to be made was still there."

I think I was supposed to be happy, but I had no clue what she meant.

"Which means?"

She smiled again.

"You have an address. Here." She handed me the slip of paper.

Now I really was happy.

"Thank you. Now it's only a matter of steps till we find what we came here for" Jake looked down at me smiling.

Lilly looked at me.

"Look, you guys are not from here, so if you ever need a lift anywhere, I can lend you one. I have a car and it would be awesome to help you out on this."

I nodded. "Definitely, maybe we might need a ride to this address."

Her eyes lit up.

"Well, you guys better get going. It's closing hour, which means trainees gotta get out." She picked up her bag. "But I put my number on the address paper, so call me anytime if you need help."

*

It was already dark out when we left the hospital. Jake took my hand and began swinging it.

"Hey, so there is this place close by to the hotel and it's called Cobble Road. There are tons of shops and little restaurants." He looked at me. "So I decided to go make a reservation at one of the finest restaurants over there. It is dress and bow tie only, so better get your fancy on."

I knew there was something coming. Where my fate was somehow me landing up in a dress not chewing too loudly. Then again I was going to see Jake in a tux. Yeah, wasn't going to pass that up.

"Wow." I stopped. "I really don't know what to say I . . . I."

"I'll take a thank you, a hug, a squeal, and a kiss."

"Thank you." I smiled genuinely, not the fake ones you do while taking a picture but a real one, a happy one.

*

Rose definitely went all-out trying to get me some clothes. There was only one dress though. Ah, she knows me too well. I laid the short black sleeveless dress on the bed, inspecting every detail. It was beautiful, simple. No sparkles, not tight, and didn't make me look like a slut. I slipped on the dress feeling the softness of the skirt tickle my thighs. My hair was softly waved tumbling down my shoulders and stopping at my elbows. Now it was time to cake a bunch of makeup on my face. I took a plastic tube of mascara and ever so carefully not to poke my eye out, I painted my eyelashes with a thin coat of black. Rose would be so proud of me right now. Now it was time for lips—.

A knock came from the door. I squeezed the tube of the clear lip stuff and splattered that on my mouth. I would totally suck at art. Jake walked in dressy shirt and pants with a tie. Dammit, no tux. Eh whatever, he still looked mighty fine. Like a cover model for Michael Kors undaroos.

"Wow." Jake came closer. "Looking good, Blue Eyes."

Phew.

"Thank you." I was already blushing, and we weren't at the restaurant yet.

He kept looking at my face. Oh shit, did I put too much lip gloss? Yeah, that's what it was. Did I accidentally paint my eyebrows black?

"Ready to go?"

I nodded.

"You might want to wear shoes." He began smiling with his too-handsome facial features. God, I was falling hard core.

I kind of walked to the closet taking out flats that looked like they would go with the dress and then walked back to him. He slipped his arm around my waist walking me out.

*

Cobble Road was full of life, adults and kids, with cars roaming everywhere. Lights were flashing, smells I'd never smelled, saxophones playing tunes from the '90s. It was perfect. Jake was perfect. I was happy, something that I hadn't been for a while. I just wanted to go run and eat everything. Okay, that was a bit disturbing.

"Ready, love? We shall dine at the finest, just us." The British accent was back and corny as ever.

We began walking toward a restaurant, lights dim. Hmm, he wasn't joking when he said dress and bow tie. A woman began laughing, wineglass swerving in the air, everyone was caught up in their own conversations. A waiter a lot older than us walked over, a friendly smile on his face.

"Do you have a reservation?" He opened a large leather book, the binding going through some crackling action.

Jake rested his hands on my waist.

"Yes, it should be under the name Jake Waterson."

The man's finger skimmed the paper and smiled.

"I see." He popped two menus. "If you please follow me."

We began walking, the smell of food making my nose weak. Right in the middle of the restaurant was a large glass circle leading outside. Trees with lights vining up the branches showing great matinees, black tables and chairs with people sitting in them were everywhere. He placed the menus lightly on a table with a small flower on one of the seats. I took about to land my tush on the chair.

"Oh no, no, no, miss you will be sitting here." The man pointed at the seating where the flower and chocolate was neatly laid on the plate.

Say what now? I looked at the mastermind Jake. Now he was going for the brownie points, not that he earned a lot already. I got up and began walking toward the other chair eyeing Jake on the process. All he did was smile. I smelled the beautifully shaped rose. Its petals were all different yet together made up something so beautiful and significant.

"Your waiter will be here shortly, hope you enjoy your meals." He winked at me and began trotting off checking on other tables.

Jake leaned into the table a little placing his arms on the top.

"So like the place?" He kept looking at me.

"Hmm" I pretended to check out the place "Um, it's okay."

I gave him the spoiled child voice, and he started to laugh. A man arrived flipping some glasses and taking some silverware and then pouring some water. Condensation immediately frosted the fancy schmancy glass surface.

"So tell me about your parents." I had been playing with my hands, my nervous habit.

"Well." He began "I told you my parents are lawyers. They are pretty famous and always have a lot of cases."

"But why did you have to come to New York? Honestly, I heard it's pretty nice in Florida."

He began looking at me and smiled leaning forward. This is a perfect example when I actually care if my breath smells okay.

"My parents wanted me to kind of get into writing, but."

Now I was officially knees deep in this story.

"But?" I waved my hand around urging him to get on and not murder me the tenseness of waiting.

"But I love art. I feel like that's something that I excel at so much more."

Art. Writing. Mr. Benson.

"Remember when Mr. Benson was giving that lecture about how writing and art is the same? It's just not same." He looked pretty frustrated. "See, some pictures don't need words and vice versa and somehow meaning that they are not the same."

I nodded, but really nodded, I completely understood everything he felt. I may not have had a mother or father who would be the main person to prone that behavior, but I am a person living in a world with those who think they are helping you climb the ladder but instead throwing you off. Sorry you had to visualize that.

*

We were walking down the cobbled road that now was basically empty. The food was good, no great, actually fantabulous. We were hand in hand laughing so hard that we actually had to stop for a few minutes. The sound of music echoed through the street, notes and melodies stringing together in perfect rhythm.

"Hey, can we go check out the music?" I looked up to him.

He smiled and bent down to kiss me on the cheek. Yep, wasn't expecting that, which could probably be noticed due to the shit-eating grin that was probably on my face.

"Of course we can, Blue Eyes."

Not sure if I should listen to what he just said or what he just did. We began walking, getting closer to the melody until we could distinguish the song. There were already a few couples sitting around listening. A guy older than us, probably in college, was the one creating the beautiful music from a violin. Jake sat down on one of those high ledges, tucking me under his shoulder. The songs changes, and Ed Sheeran's "Thinking Out Loud" began jumping off the strings. The warmth along the side of my body was taken away.

"Will you take this dance, Blue Eyes?" He did the whole hand-swishing-asking thing. When he did that, how could I say no?

"I will not be held accountable if some bone in your body is broken." He raised his brow. I raised my hands in surrender as we walked to the middle of the sidwalkish area. "Just putting in out there."

He put my arm on his shoulder, and his hand fit like a puzzle piece on my waist.

"Maybe just the touch of a hand."

Apparently, I was supposed to spin but I looked like a spazzed out fish. He just started laughing, which didn't help at all. But soon after I joined in, at least it think I did, we began swaying and a lot of spinning and eye to eye contact. The music gradually began going softer, but the dancing was still hard core 'cause I was sweating like a donkey while my partner looked flawless like the people from *Dancing with the Stars*. Jake dipped me, the swoosh of air doing funny things to my head moving tiny pieces of hair out of my face. The music went softer and softer with every sway and spin. And stopped with another dip. The sounds of clapping replaced the music. I looked around. Apparently other people came to dance as well. The boy took a bow. A woman came over and was on the verge of dropping a dollar bill in his case, but he refused. He said something to the women, and she smiled walking back to her friend. Money still crumpled up in the palms of hand. I nudged Jake to come.

"You were amazing." I looked down, the boy was packing the instrument up. He stood up and smiled at me.

"Thanks, you are really good at dancing." He winked moving his hair away from his eyes.

Oh, this would be a great payback from the hospital. If only I knew where Jake was.

"Ha, I am definitely not a good dancer, but really you're good at playing. It probably was really hard to learn."

Jake came trotting, smiling, and nodding his head at the boy. That didn't go as planned.

"Sometimes." He shuffled his feet. "But I just went by a metaphor my grandfather told me when I was learning. Never give up because that is the same thing as surrendering in a battle." He smiled again.

What is it with everyone and their metaphor? He picked up his violin case handle and shook Jake's hand and winked at me. I could have sworn to see steam waving off from atop his head.

"Well, it was nice meeting you, guys. Have a nice remainder of your trip." He waved and began walking, his base carpenter shoes dragging along.

Then again, was it that obvious that we were tourist? I didn't even take a selfie, not one.

"You jellies?" I felt the urge to taunt him.

"Always I prefer not to share." He took my hand mocking the wink the music boy gave. Okay, he might have exaggerated a bit. "Ready to go, Blue Eyes? We have to wake up early to get Lilly to give us a ride."

I nodded, and we walked back onto the cobbled rode, which reminded me of a little line from my favorite story.

"There's no place like home."

*

I brushed my knotted hair out, tying it into a messy bun on the top of my head. This was definitely the night I'll remember for a long time. The night I danced for romance. That was catchy. Like a little kid, I cannonballed into the bed, lying my head on the plush feathery pillows and cocooning myself in the white cotton sheets. I squirmed a bit, promising myself that I wasn't going to move. But I couldn't stop. I wasn't tired. It's 11:55 p.m. I didn't want to disturb Jake. There was nothing else to do but to dream how would my mother be like, smart, tall, funny, nice . . .

*

I woke up with the worst nightmare, sweat pouring off my forehead seeping into the puffy blanket, tears running down my cheeks. My newest worst nightmare hit me, hit me hard. What if I don't find them, what if they don't want me to find them? I padded into the bathroom clutching the rim of the sink till my knuckles turned white. Slowly lifting my head, I stared into the eyes of the beast that was waiting to unravel itself from the pool of yarn that somehow managed to just keep shortening. My cheeks stained from the salty tears that seemed not to end and eyes bloodshot like I'd taken drugs. I guess this was a relapse of sadness. The kind were you take too little, and it comes back with an army. All I know is that I was curled up in a ball, crying, then I was running out the door, key in my back pocket.

The weather was strange. Though it was immensely hot during the day, it's surprisingly cold during the night. I began running down the street, puffs of white smoke tailing along with every breath I took. The coldness reminded me of home, the home I was spoon fed to be true. My heels dug into the ground pushing me off as I started running faster. The scenery wasn't much, a man decided to drink his misery swaying through the night, laughing like hyena. Well, at least he was smiling. My temples throbbed as I turned the corner, which brought me back to the rotating door of the hotel. Running away from my problems seemed to work. Literally and figuratively. 'Cause if you run far enough, your problem will be too small to be visible.

For a short while that is.

*

I had been daydreaming for the rest of the morning until I decided to finally go wake up the sleeping beauty. The room was dark and warm. To my surprise, it was actually pretty tidy. Excluding the side coffee table, which were scattered with charcoaled pencil drawing. Or it might have been black crayon. Most of the blanket was pooled off the bed onto the ground, but under the remainder of the blanket that was on the bed was Jake. Shirtless with pajama pants, chiseled chest peacefully rising and falling. He looked relaxed. Well, everything has an end. I slid in the bed in a standing-up position.

This was going to be fun.

I began jumping as hard as I could on the bed, avoiding any head to wall contacts. He began tossing and turning. This actually would be an awesome wake-up call option, except for it being kind of creepy if someone you didn't know just casually walked in and began jumping on your bed. Finally, hazel orbs were staring right at me.

"What kind of wake-up call is this?" He began laughing.

I smiled, sliding off the bed. "The fun kind."

He slid of the bed stretching, stomach smoothing out. Talk about distracting.

"Okay, well, we need to text Lilly for that ride to that address." He began walking to the table leaning against it.

"Go put a shirt on. Your stomach is distracting, and I already called her."

He smiled.

"Seems like you woke up early."

"Yep."

I walked out the room giving him time to get dressed and ready for the day ahead.

*

Lilly owned a ridgy old red Nissan truck. But if its engine was going, so was I. We were walking out the hotel when we saw her car parked in the lot out back, and she was leaning on it scrolling through her phone.

"Hey." She slipped the pink-cased iPhone in her back pocket.

"Thanks again for giving us the ride."

She nodded walking toward the driver's seat. She opened the door and swung in, making it look like some easy shit, but when I tried, my shoe might have gotten stuck in the gap between the car and the foot railing thing. There were CDs of rock songs dumped everywhere. I was almost positive I sat on one.

"Sorry about all the CDs. I was initially going to major in music, but my parents were putting me down for it saying that they did not raise a rock star." She shrugged it off like it was no big deal.

The tiredness from the early morning run decided to hit me now. I looked out the window as we coasted off a highway into a more woodsy area, tons of ferns and pine trees with assorted colors.

"What kind of music do you normally listen to?" Jake leaned back.

"Well, normally rock, but I make my own mixes. Some of the CDs are my mix tapes. Just gotta dig around." She opened up the dashboard taking out a scratched up CD handing it to Jake. "I am taking a lot of electives on music at school, but yeah, what about you two?"

I wasn't in the mood of sharing my life story right now, going to a random address not knowing whose life you're about to step in is a lot more nerve racking than it seemed. But I think that Jake has a pretty good handle on answering questions than I do. For the rest of the ride, I ignored the constant arguing about who should have won the EMAs and paid attention to the view. California had never struck me as a woodsy kind of place, but more of a city. Like Mr. Benson used to say, to assume makes you into an ass. He wasn't wrong, the thought of everyone at home came back to me like a wave to the shore. How is Cook doing, is she that tough New Yorker, or even Rose, how is her vacation going? I think the correct term for the feelings I was going through was good old homesickness. The car began going deeper into the trees until it stopped in front of a house. I was getting the *Cabin in the Woods* vibes right about now. There was a red pickup Ford parked in the front. It was a small house, probably two stories yet so isolated from the city life outside. I opened the door last still looking at the house.

"Well, here we are." Lilly looked at the house then at me with a short crooked smile.

I nodded.

"Do you want me to come, Blue Eyes?" His hand was on my shoulder, green eyes more on the brown side peering at me.

"No, I . . . I want to do this alone." I turned and looked at both of them. "Please."

All they did was nod and watch me. I walked onto the gravel path and onto the wooden steps leading up to the porch. Well, here goes nothing. Who am I kidding? Here goes everything. I knocked. Nothing. Hmm, that's not what I expected. I knocked again. Okay, well, this is awkward. I began walking back down the stairs nodding my head.

"Can I help you?" I turned around to see a woman at the doorstep. She was pretty in her early thirties.

But she looks nothing like me. Is she my mother?

"Um yes, I need to ask some questions. My name is Ash Kaiden Rowe." Her green eyes widened for a second then went back to normal size.

"I . . . come in." She held out the screen door, and I stepped inside. "Take off your shoes right there."

The house was small but cozy. There was a fireplace in the back with a sofa and a couple of chair around it. It smelt like cake from one of those Yankee candles, but there were a lot of paintings like everywhere, some on easels that were yet to be completed and others on tables.

"Please sit. I'll be right back." I sat on the black sofa that my butt sunk right into.

The lady came back with a pitcher full of lemonade and two glasses. She moved a couple of paintings out of the way and placed the yellow drink atop the table.

"Lemonade?" I nodded she tipped the pitcher "You have grown so big since the last I've seen you. You look beautiful just like your mother." So this lady is not my mother.

"You know my mother?" I sipped the tangy sweet liquid.

"Yes, yes, I did. I'm Lydia by the way." She looked at me. "She's still alive, we've lost contact for years."

I didn't know what to say or do. I1 just nodded.

"She love—"

"Don't." My throat felt like someone was choking me. "If she loved me, she would have come back, but she never did."

She said nothing but looked at me and smiled.

"So what brings you here?" She put down her drink. "And how did you ever get my address? I thought Amber had blocked everything off."

Amber. So that was her name, my mother's name. Amber Rowe.

"I went to my birth hospital. Everything was blocked off except this address, so . . ."

She nodded, looking at a piece of lint on the floor.

"Amber was my best friend during high school. We were literally always together, morning, night didn't matter. We decided that we would get this house and stay here as our own place when we went to college. But things changed, choices were made, and they were so bad that we never talked again. After a while, I heard that she dropped out of college that we went to together and enrolled into a new one. People made speculations and rumors." She straightened her legs. "But it was hard to know which was a faux or fact. I haven't heard anything to this day."

"What kind of choices?" I looked at her hard, going over every detail of her face.

"Not my story to tell, kid, not my story to tell."

Well, that helps. I got up and looked at the side table. There was a book. It was black and said High School Yearbook on it.

"Do you mind?" I showed the book to her.

"Ah, I almost forgot, that is the yearbook. There is a picture of Amber somewhere in there."

I flipped to the A. There I saw it. It was a girl about my age, same hair color as me but darker eyes and a fifty-watt smile. She was pretty.

"All the boys used to swoon about her. She was really good in school and everything, always did extra stuff. We loved painting. She won a lot of competitions. I remember every Saturday, there was a gallery. No matter what weather, she wouldn't miss it." She chuckled as if the whole movie was playing back in her mind.

STA. School of the Arts.

"I should get going. Do you mind if I could take this with me?" I looked at her hopefully.

"Sure." She got up walking me to the door. "Not like I need it anyway. Good luck finding her. Don't have high expectations of her though, not after you hear the whole story."

What was so bad about this story? I went down the stairs looking back at the house. Jake and Lilly were talking by the car with hopeful faces when I came, but I said nothing, just went into the car. I wasn't about to exploit my plan just yet.

*

"Well." Jake ran his fingers through his hair "What's this mastermind plan?"

He was sitting cross legged on the couch, Lilly sitting next to him.

"Okay, so when I was there, I found some . . . information about my mother."

I looked at them.

"Which is." Lilly stared at me like the answer was written on my forehead or something.

"So they were both friends in high school, they bought that house together to initially stay when they go to college. But she said something about choices that were made which were so bad that . . ." I didn't realize that I was up and pacing. "Made them separate and lose all contact, and apparently she had moved out of the house. But she is still in California."

Jake looked at me. Well, officially I know that I suck at silent emphasis. I'm guessing it's given as a God-gifted talent.

"But I was looking at Lydia's side table, and I saw this." I pointed to the yearbook that seeped into the blanket.

"Wait." Now Lilly was pacing. "If you saw their yearbook, then that means you must have seen the picture and name of your mother."

I nodded.

"And since she officially attended the high school, then there could be her emergency contact information."

"Which may not get me exactly to my mother, but to someone else."

"Who would probably know your mother and give us some info like . . ."

"Lydia." I think Jake started to feel lonely.

All I could do was smile. This reminded me of Scooby Doo. Chasing after something that just keeps running.

*

The same nightmare hit me where my mother didn't want me to find her, but this time I didn't run. I was tired of running from my problems. I stood up allowing the darkness of the room to embrace me, while the cold tears numbed. Shadow danced on the wall from the buildings outside the hotel. That's it. I could just sit there and do nothing. A paper was on my desk and luckily the hotel branded pen was there too. The tears that couldn't be explained by water went on that paper. God dammit, this didn't help either. I crumpled the paper frustratingly throwing across the room. The black yearbook just remained harmlessly on the table, like seriously just lying there and taunting me. So now I was looking through the yearbook, yay.

Amber Rowe.

Everything fit together perfectly yet so imperfectly. The argument that somehow included me and my welfare. Choices that we probably made in a bad manner. These stupid choices that affect my childhood, how I grew up. Every birthday, every graduation. Every breath. I threw the book across the room. It banged off the wall thumping onto the floor. I hope these walls were soundproof. The door that connected Jake's and my room was closed, so just hoping he doesn't have Spidey senses or something. Well, I was officially bored and pissed. What a mix! I got up and walked to the door and knocked.

"Come in, Blue Eyes."

Well, he said okay. I slid the key in the atomic key checker and walked in. Jake and in pj's was sitting on the bed, scrolling through channels on the TV. He then switched it off scooting back and patted the side of the bed.

"Don't worry, I got my cooties vaccination." I threw him a troll face glare and sat on the similar bed to mine. "So what brings you into my majestic bedroom that so happens to belong to the hotel?"

Now how can I stay pissed and bored when he keeps talking to me like that.

"For starters, I am feeling bored, pissed, sad, and scared." I began playing with my hands. They seemed a lot more fun than admitting my feelings at this point.

He smiled and took out a pencil and paper.

"Why are you feeling like this?"

I fell back.

"I am scared I won't be able to find her or possibly them and worse that they don't me to find them. I mean after everything we've seen, clearly they wanted to be out of my life. But still it's just everything. All my emotions are like circling about what that stupid argument was!"

I turned around so I was facing him, but he was just drawing. A misted forest.

"Well. We're doing everything we can, and you know what, if it was supposed to happen, great. If not, to hell with it."

"I know that, but—"

"No buts. Why do not we just distract ourselves from this. Remember we are still on vacation. Put this aside and take a new picture." He put the drawing aside. "A little birdie told me that Dory was a little something to you."

He kissed my cheek and smiled. I smiled back rolling over so that I was in a seal position. Rose and I were obsessed with *Finding Nemo*. The obsession increased to the point where we memorized every line word per word.

"Does this little birdy so happen to have blue hair and will never miss bite fest?"

"If that means that, she's my smoking hot girlfriend's best friend, then yes, yes, she did."

"Really?" I got up snuggling close.

"Now why would I lie to you?" He scrolled to the hotels on-demand thing.

We watched the movie. Forgetting about the world, letting it do its own thing while we did ours.

*"If I just lay here, if I just lay here,
would you lie with me and just forget the world?"*

*

I guess we just fell asleep while watching the movie. I woke up peering around the dark room, yep, still in Jake's room, which I totally didn't mind. The TV was still on advertising a very modest man holding "the best soap in the world." I got up, and throwing the covers off in the most nonthrowing way, the lump on the other side of the bed stirred; he looked like a mutated cat. Hah, I am so going to make fun of him on that. I smiled and slipped through the door. Everything was set like how it was last night, paper all over my desk, some crumpled, others just there, and the yearbook half opened lying on the other side of the room from the desk's point of view. It was only 5:45 a.m., so I could just buy some time to myself. Cook always made fun of me saying I wasn't a normal teen who would sleep late and get up twice the times later. I picked up the yearbook and cleared off the papers on the desk. Ah, I need a bath. Even though there was a big tub in the bathroom, I haven't taken advantage of it. Don't worry I took showers every day, even scrubbed in between my fingers. I removed my pj's pampering myself with a puffy white robe, yeah, Rose be tripping. And so I basically started my morning by playing with soapsuds and watching my fingers and toes wrinkle.

*

I creepingly walked into the connecting room sitting on the small coffee table and stocked the mutated cat in the blanket. The table was still scattered with tons of different papers and his laptop, and there was that charcoaled pencil drawing of a girl.

"You know that's you, right?"

"Holy shit." I swung around punching him square in the nuts. I swear I didn't mean too but self-defense, ya know.

I threw the drawing at the table bending down.

"Oh my gosh, I am so sorry, holy crap." He looked at me like he had drunken a bottle of champagne and going through the disgusting aftershock.

All I could do was flat out laughing rolling all over the floor. I'm almost positive my shirt took care of the cleaning lady's job.

"Okay, I think I'm good." He regained himself. "And thanks for your help, Blue Eyes, I'm going in the bathroom. I have a morning breath."

"Yes, yes, you do."

The sound of the tap abruptly began to flow so I went back to my room the get the yearbook. We have some research to do 'cause right off the bat, the school was pretty professional, meaning they wouldn't buy the idea of me looking for my mother. On the front page was a picture of the school, it was clean looking not like our school. Jake came out of the bathroom wiping his hands on a towel.

"So what do you think we should do, oh wise one?" Well, he wasn't wrong about that.

"Well, I think we should possibly research first. See if it's still around 'cause it is kinda old." Then again it would really suck donkey balls if it weren't.

"I actually had breakfast in mind, but that works too."

I laughed.

"Come on, I'm hungry too."

*

I stuffed a piece of toast as elegantly as I could without embarrassing myself 'cause I think the elderly couple was staring at me. We were in the lobby lounge that apparently serves free breakfast. Jake was enjoying a super intricate breakfast.

"Have you ever thought"—he played with a piece of rosemary that garnished his platter—"how much passion people have?"

Hm.

"For example, to make this dish, you can't just slap stuff on it and call it perfection." He looked at the plate and at me.

"That's where I believe the passion comes from."

"But where does the passion come from?"

I looked at him. I am utterly and definitely confused.

"The passion comes from goals and dedication."

He smiled, which is weird 'cause I have like no clue what's going on or where this is leading to.

"Yes, but where does the goals and dedication come from?"

Seriously?

"Well, obviously perseverance from themselves and also parents."

"See, here's the thing." He tossed a minitomato around the dish. "A parent can only reinforce their kid so much, but at the end, it is a talent that is gifted, and the universal question is who gifts it."

I am still so confused, but I nodded. My phone started to vibrate successfully grabbing my attention as the fork went hurdling toward the ground. Well, at least it was someone I wanted to talk to. Lilly.

"Hello." I rested the phone on my shoulder.

"So what's the next plan?"

"To devour the rest of my Californian style French toast." I popped a piece of the sweet bread into my mouth.

"Great," some more shuffling. "I'm in the lobby, and we are altering that plan."

I laughed at the urgency in her voice, but a queasy feeling settled in the bottom of my stomach.

"Who was it?" Jake took a swing of his orange juice.

"Oh, was just Lilly, she's coming to the hotel to discuss about the plan, so she's kind of in the lobby."

"Well, logically, we should probably go there before she punches the poor man at the reception desk." He stretched smiling. "But sadly my legs don't obtain common logic, so."

I put my napkin on the table picking up Betsy and giving her a good swing over my shoulder.

"Well, tell your legs to get the up before hell breaks loose in the lobby." I offered my hand. He took it encasing it with his softness and warmth.

We walked out into the lobby to find Lilly in the corner tapping her foot urgently. She was wearing a short-sleeved crop top paired with shorts and flats. Hm, stylish. She had a backpack on and a bunch of papers in her hand which looked like they were going to drop any minute.

"Here, lemme help with that."

"Oh my gosh, there you are! What took you so long?" She half dropped, half handed the papers to me.

"My legs." Jake looked at us completely undeterred by what the legit just said.

Lilly's shaped brow went up. And my cheeks blazed up like a heater.

"Okay, that sounded so wrong."

"No shit, Sherlock." Lilly flipped her hair. "'Kay, well, are ya guys ready or not, 'cause I want to give you some breathing time before I knock your flip-flops off."

Jake laughed at that. I mean, honestly, for the short time of knowing Lilly, that is most definitely something she would say. Without grinning. Like what?

"I think it's knock your socks off?"

"It's like a billion degrees outside, like honestly you're gonna blaze like a firework if you are even planning to wear any socks."

*

We were all sitting in my room, on the made bed, relaxed. On the other hand, Lilly was knocking her flip-flops off a whole lot more.

"Okay, okay, okay, well, I did some research on the high school, and I found tons of stuff." She gave me a paper. "So luckily, the high school is still up and doing pretty good, it's only for the prestigious Arts students, including dancing, singing, theater, writing, and regular boring art." She waved her arm around and looked at her highlighted paper.

Wait, so that means that both Lydia and my mom attended this school. For boring arts meaning that she had to be very smart and highly educated and a round-about smarty pants.

"Yeah, Lydia did say something about my mom being a dedicated art student, used to love it." I felt like I was mourning.

She nodded going back to the paper.

"I checked out the tuition fee, and damn, you could buy a maserati with that amount of money. And also since it is costing money, we might get another name or an address similar to a hospital."

"That's awesome, then it'll be ten times easier, but again this still stands by if they'll give us an address or anything." Jake stretched lying back, fiddling around with the remote for the TV.

"Well yeah, and one more thing, they have a different schedule than public school, meaning they are open during our winter break, so they will be open this whole week. Oh, and they're closed on weekends, so they'll be open tomorrow."

"Okay, well, now we know our next step." Jake put his arm around my waist, pulling me closer, his shirt smelling of soap and a lemony cologne.

"Hey, do you guys wanna come over tonight for some pizza and video games?" She flashed puppy dog eyes and looked like she was going to jump up and down.

"We don't have anything else to do." Jake looked down at me and smiled. "Sure, but it's only eleven in the morning."

"Psh yeah, so you two spend some time together. Go do some sightseeing 'cause my shift at the hospital starts in like twenty minutes anyhow, so I better get going."

She popped up like a female temperamental Jack-in-the-box, gathered her things dumping them into her backpack.

"'Kay, well, I'll text ya when my shift's over, and you can come over! Bye!" She ran out of the room.

That went well. I looked back at Jake who was simply smiling and shaking his head.

"I don't even know how to comment to that so I am just going to stick to ignoring."

Well, that was definitely one thing to do about it. But then again, Lilly was the kind of character in a book who was probably the hardest to figure out. Honestly, she's either a ghetto or a princess. Ha ghetto-princess.

"So what's the plans for today, oversized cat?" I rolled on the bed kicking my feet in the air.

His eyebrow shot up, yet he smiled.

"Well, I was thinking that we should go check out the pool, Blue Eyes." He played with my hair, twirling it around his finger. "If that's okay with you, my writing genius."

"I don't mind. I was actually hoping to go check it out anyway."

"Plus it will give me a chance to see you in a bathing suit." He laughed when I tried to slap him on his arm.

*

"I swear, if you don't jump in with me right now, I am quite willing to drag your cute butt into the pool!"

We were at the pool already. The sun was blazing, and it was actually really hot outside Which gave a pretty logical excuse for the pool people, to make it below a thousand degrees.

"I'm not coming in! It's way too cold!" I crossed my arms around my chest impersonating a whiney kid.

"You asked for it!"

He threw me over his shoulder and plummeted into the water. Yeah, I was feeling pretty cold right about now. Thanks to my awesome duck skills, I floated steadily, my hair dripping. When I was about ten Rose would invite me to her pool, then was the time when I was convinced that I could wish hard enough and be gifted with the power of breathing underwater. By the way, just to keep the record straight, the ability was never given to me. A hand grabbed my leg and I was pulled back underwater by the shark named Jake. His hair was everywhere, but his lips were on mine. And no superpower or ability could be better than that kiss. Nothing ever. There was no deep breathing. It wasn't under the moonlight. Wasn't forced. Wasn't perfect.

That was my first kiss. It was mine. Just mine.

*

You know in those cheesy novels where the girl would turn into mush by just simply looking at this Mr. perfect? I was totally becoming into one. And honestly, this is a serious problem because I have never experienced that. As a matter of fact, I have never experienced smiling as much as I had during the course of this trip, as well as something that seemed to be so ordinary to others which was an airplane. It seemed strange, how sometimes when a new experience is introduced into a person's palette. It resembles the feeling of walking for the first time. I walked out from the bathroom tying the towel encasing my wet hair, like a cocoon if you must. Tonight we were going over to the fire bender with an impeccable taste of fashion den, also known as Lilly's house.

For some reason I felt a little awkward, now that we had our first kiss, things would change. I heard some shuffling from the other side, then the door flung open, and a smiling Jake dressed in a muscle tee with California displayed on the front and those drawstring shorts.

"You're such a dork. You have a key, you know." He began to slightly chuckle.

"Hey, trying to be considerate of your modesty." We began walking down the hotel hallway. "By the way, I think wearing that shirt is a big tourist move."

He shrugged.

"Well, at least I'm representing."

*

Lilly's house wasn't too big nor too small but just in the middle. It was the kind that gave off the good vibe sense. Meaning that in that mediocre house, nothing wasn't used over two times for different tasks. Her family was honestly the best part. Her mom was so kind, always asked if we needed anything and was ready to tend to us, and to Lilly that was annoying. But for me, it was something that was lacked so very much in my life.

"What do your parents do?" Jake stretched out next to me taking a swing of his coke.

Lilly was up fiddling around with the controllers for the Xbox trying to get *Call of Duty* up with all our profile names.

"Well, my dad is a criminal justice lawyer and my mom is a nurse. She's off for this week, but she does like night shifts and stuff. So basically she's asleep during the day."

"That's awesome." For some apparent reason, she always complained about her parents' jobs, but they didn't seem bad to me.

"Not really, they go under a shitload of stress, and then on top of that, my parents want me to get into medical." She plopped onto the shiny black couch recliner thing, handing us both a controller. "Plus sometimes it's hard trying to prove yourself when they put such a high standard of expectation for you to meet. And they consistently compare me with my older brother Eric."

I looked at her. For some reason, everyone had their own set of issues, which varied from the large array of different spices of life. Lilly fiddled around with the joystick of the controller, there was pain in her eyes. A different kind of pain. The kind that had something to do with her dream, like someone was clipping away her wings.

"So how do we play this?" I put a smile on my face.

Lilly's eyes bulged.

"You don't know how to play zombies?" She looked like someone just told her that we had no other choice but to move to the moon.

"Nope, we don't have an Xbox in the orphanage." I began laughing as she tried taking it all in.

"Okay, you're like a Martian." She moved closer explaining each control.

*

Nope, most definitely not easy at all. I ate at least my fourth slice of pizza, okay, okay fifth, fine, the whole pie and a half a bottle of soda. And yet I went down at least twenty times in a round, and it was also pretty obvious that Lilly was going to fork her eyes out, and when a fork is involved in a removal of a body part, it is pretty serious. Honestly I was having the time of my life. For the first time, I soaked in the moment and let the rest slip through like sand. Jeez I was becoming so senti. We finally had enough with shooting things, so we began to talk.

"So for tomorrow, I am going to be picking you guys at around five." She looked from me to Jake. "What's the matter? You look like someone ran over your favorite puppy."

"Um, well, you see, I don't look this good in the morning unless I do have a proper beauty sleep." Jake gave the whole hair flip motion.

How could you not laugh at that? We basically had the whole plan set out, but plans are nothing unless they work. And sadly I don't have a full functioning crystal ball that could tell me past, present, or future. But really that, all we need is a crystal ball dictating the past. All of the past.

*

"If this is some senior prank, you understand you could get into a lot of trouble."

"We assure you, miss, this isn't a prank." Jake said he is literally blessed with his people skills. "If you just please let us talk to the principal."

The secretary looked at us unbelievingly. Honestly I couldn't blame her, but she really needed an attitude check. She drummed her really long and fake nails against her droopy cheek.

"You do have evidence to support that you guys are actually trying to do whatever you're doing? Principal Regan is a very busy woman, you know." Her eyebrow shot up.

That's it! This is a perfect time where my antisocial behavior might save us all.

"Look, lady, all we are trying to do is find my mom, and this is one of the big steps we need to take. All we want is a little time with the principal to discuss some stuff, so if you please." I splayed my hand on the shiny desk.

She stared at me for a little while, then clicked a button on the black phone.

"She's ready for you." Miss Puckerpuss moved some papers around her desk. "Down the hall to the right. I recommend you knock before you enter."

Lilly began walking and I trailed behind her.

"I want to kiss your feet in awe." Lilly looked at me. "You didn't hear that from me."

Less than a moment went by as I stared at the glossy brown door, which I may add was two hundred times better than the lifeless grey doors that the high school back home had. My knuckles curled. Going once, going twice.

"Come in."

I completely froze. A warm hand was placed on my shoulder.

"It's okay, just go in. It will be fine. I am here," Jake whispered to me.

I nodded and opened the door. The room was big, like really big. The basic color scheme was brown. There was a big painting of a woman which I'm expecting was the principal.

"Um." The women kept typing on the computer.

"Please take a seat." Her eyes shot up for a split second. "All of you."

I sat down a bit uncomfortably. There was a steel name tag on the front of the desk. Ms. Romebotham. Still single I wonder why. The lady looked ancient. She lifted her hand to click her laptop close.

"So what is it that you are here today in our high school?" She folded her aged hands, which looked so incredibly squishy.

"You see, I came to California for a chance to find my mother. After a whole lot of stuff, we came to find out that my mother attended this high school." I peeked at her. Her eyes reminded me of a snake, Voldemort to be exact.

She twisted a heavy-looking steel pen. Hm, even the writing instruments are topnotch here.

"Do you," she waved her hand around the pen still nestled in between her fingers, "Have some sort of, let's say, photograph or possibly a date of when your relation has attended this school?"

Literally, English would work, but I was almost positive this meant that the yearbook. If not, this was about to get a whole lot awkward. I opened up Betsy and took out the yearbook. I fell asleep yesterday night just reading the whole memorandum so I made sure to doggy flap the page where my mom's photo was. She took the book pulling up her specs that dangled from those cheesy yet most likely real small pearl chain draped around her neck, examining the picture. I could have sworn that her wrinkled red-pigmented lips lifted just a tiny millimeter.

"I knew you were a Rowe from the beginning." She looked at me smiling. "Your mother was an amazing student. Extraordinarily gifted in the group criteria of painting arts. From the beginning, I knew she was going to do very well because she had you. A beautiful girl." Well, wasn't expecting that. She turned from a noseless creature to a sugarplum fairy go figure.

"So . . . will you help us?" Lilly shifted next to me. Honestly, this was the most quiet that she had ever been.

The principal looked at all of us. And nodded.

"Yes, I will," she removed the specs letting it take its place back on her neck, "but what do you actually need?"

Showtime.

"Since she did attend this school, she had to take a standardized test of some sort." Now she was looking at me like I had grown a second head."

"Yes. The point is?" Her lips puckered, and creases of concentration marred her forehead.

"To take a standardized test, you must have basic background knowledge. Plus the school might have needed emergency contacts information or an address of some sort." I looked hopefully at her, who had an impeccable amount of concentration.

I felt moments pass by, which was completely silent, until Ms. Romebotham got up from her chair and walked to the door. Well, that's it, we were getting kicked out of this school and possibly California. At least I'll remember that.

"Follow me please." Her heels tapped onto the marble like hallway, her posture like a beam. "We are taking a trip to the grading room. We opened the school around the time your mother joined. Therefore her old grading stuff might still be in there." She turned around, her words punctuating.

She took out a chain of dangling keys, picking out a golden lustering key, and slipped it through the hole hearing the click of success. The room was much more organized than the monstrosity in the hospital, everything neatly arranged in labeled boxes.

"Here we go." She pulled out the box with the same date that was printed on the yearbook. "Whatever is in here is the criteria that was mandatory to bring in and allow the school to keep during that time period."

She flipped through the alphabets to K pulling out the most wanted file.

"It's all yours." She handed the dark blue folder in my hands, which was shaking so hard it resembled an earthquake. "If you find what you want, just let me know. You aren't allowed to leave with an original copy of anything, so the secretary will make a copy for you. I will be right outside." With that, she walked out the room leaving the door open.

This was it. I opened the folder peering at all the papers. Most were written in script. But that wasn't what I was looking for. I flipped through the pages, then stopped at a small slip, an emergency nurse form. An address, a bloody address. In black print. I probably didn't notice or didn't care to acknowledge a fat cold tear sliding down my face.

"Blue Eyes." Jake came around taking the folder out of my spaghetti and sweaty fingers. "It's okay, we . . . we will find another way."

I shook my head.

"No."

"What do you mean?" He ran his finger across the tear, essentially terminating it.

"An address, a bloody address!"

He smiled, a big fat goofy smile. And then there was a snort.

"Yeah, yeah, I love, I love you too." They ate each other's faces off. "So shall we get this address copied?" Lilly swooshed her hands to the door.

I laughed taking Jake's hand, which had no trouble holding my hand.

*

We walked into the main office. Ms. Puckerpuss had a smile as bright as a block of cheese that hasn't been cut, but you could visible see the large icicles falling from each chemically whitened tooth.

"Okay, so I'll take that, honey, and get you a copy, so you can be on your merry way." She pivoted around walking in a straight line, not even swaying a bit.

I turned to Lilly.

"I think a sugarplum fairy from hell pissed in her coffee."

"Or she got hit by an attitude check bus, honestly either works." She snorted.

The woman walked back in the room, obtaining a copy of that treasured paper. And literally I had to yank it out of her hand, slightly jealous on how well maintained they were.

"So I am guessing we are most likely going to have to go to that address as soon as possible. Of course now we are in the crunch time of this trip." Jake held his arm over my shoulder, giving it a squeeze and looking down at me.

He was right. Just one thing. This address couldn't have been any Jo Shmo 'cause a parent or guardian's number could only be there as an emergency. Meaning that this address could only be my grandparents. The old, the wistful, and a possible key. Just have to make sure the key isn't broken.

*

I was sitting on the bed and out of complete boredom, doodling on a hotel welcome card I found. And since I am a crappy artist, most of my doodles look like jumbles of disoriented objects with no significant meaning, which was fine with me. The door opened, and Jake came strolling in smiling, pulling up a chair near the bed.

"Hello, Pajama Princess," his green eyes, "was just thinking."

I rolled around on the bed so that I was facing him with my feet in the air.

"We should go for some hot chocolate." He smiled, pushing a strand of hair behind my ear.

"But it's too hot for hot chocolate."

"Well, no actually. Christmas is the day after we leave, so Saturday, and since we can't even bake cookies right now and for the sake of tradition and going out with you, let's go for some hot chocolate, Blue Eyes." His explanation was preposterous, but it was the best kind.

"Mmmm." I pretended to think with my pointer finger indenting in my cheek as if I were trying to make dimples. "Fine. Get out I am going to change."

He got up quickly kissing me, running like a mouse that stole a cookie. I put on some suitable coffee shop clothes and a bit of gloss and running my comb through my hair until I was satisfied with the results.

We were walking hand and hand down the beautiful vintage-style street. You know, with the cute little '90s malt parlors. And the barbers with the candy cane swirling cylinder thing. As of this point, I might be offending barbers worldwide. But that's okay 'cause we won't judge.

"So tell me more about your parents."

We walked into a small homey coffee shop named Lavender, which actually had nothing to do with the smell of lavender, the color, or even the actual flower. Strange. And to my surprise, they did sell hot chocolate in California.

"Go get a table and I'll order." I nodded.

The surroundings were mostly teens. Some were on dates others with laptops and headphones in, probably working on papers. Wouldn't be surprised. Jake came back, two mugs in his hand that were steaming like nuts, and thank god they had Lavender printed in white computerized ink, which was slightly fading, but I like it.

"You didn't answer the question." The hot chocolate touched my tongue, burning the everlasting crap of it, but had an amazing aftertaste.

"What question?" He took a sip, and a chocolate mustache appeared above his lip, and for the sake of people's eye candy, I didn't say a word.

"About your parents."

"I already told you they are lawyers." He folded his hands atop the table so elegantly, yet I couldn't take him seriously with the milkstache.

"But why are you here in the scenes of New York instead of Florida?"

He looked at me as if the answers were written on my face. And that's when I knew, there was something with his childhood. Something big. Something different yet not so different.

"Jake, how was your childhood like?"

He rubbed his face with the heel of his hand.

"My parents were lawyers, very wealthy ones at that. They had so much money, they never knew what to do with, and then I came. You might think this is some crappy Richie Rich story, but," he snorted and shook out the light curls in his hair, "my parents really have a blind sight to me. Always had nannies, some would even steel form the house. But who cared, at least there was somewhere the money would go."

He stopped for a little bit. I could see the pain in his eyes and how much this pulled his heart. Everything was open. He was as naive like a small child. It was so unlike him, and it tore me shred by shred.

"They were always gone, all the time. To some party here and some party there. They literally gave two ninja flying shits about me. The only good memories I had was Christmas, of course not with them but with the staff. They were awesome. We would have the best times all together, hot chocolate, games, and presents." A small smile tugged the corner of his lips. He looked into my eyes. "Then finally, my parents decided to send me to New York to my uncle's place. Out of the whole family, he was my mom and dad combined. Meanwhile my parents were all hello and bye-bye, Uncle Benson was there, and he knew what was going on. So I came here as in to New York and yeah, still there. But I have met someone who clicks my puzzle and never seizes to amaze me."

I was amazed by everything. And also partially witnessing my heart doing the marimba straight out of my chest by the last sentence.

He just was everything, and there should be nothing a person like him who should have to go through that ever.

"I love you." I looked around after a long time. No one was there, just people cleaning up putting chairs away, then looked back down to the cocoa. "I think this has become cold cocoa now."

He began to chuckle and got up taking the cups to the placement when done area.

"I think that we should probably get going before we get kicked out for partying too hard in a coffee shop."

"What?" I started to laugh at the illogicalness of the statement.

"Sorry, felt the need."

I laughed and kissed him on the cheek as we walked out of the shop, his story ringing in my ear.

*

It was early in the morning when we were back in Lilly's DVD-hoarded car. The address that was given to us at the school, after a lot of examination, was a house in North of California in Naples where the wineries were. And we were in the South, so it was going to take us about two trains and a taxi ride.

"Houses up north are actually pretty expensive." Lilly popped open the dashboard and took out two pairs of sunglasses handing me one. "Think they got a little cash money?"

"Thanks." I slid the holographic shade, which probably made me look like a fail superhero atop my nose. "Have no clue, honestly could care less."

She snorted.

"Someone woke up on the wrong side of the bed today."

"Sorry, just drowning in my thoughts."

"Calm down, you're reminding me of Ms. Perky Town from the school." She began to laugh, and I was getting scared 'cause this was Lilly.

"My bad." But I still smiled.

I looked out the fogged up window toward the lively city behind it.

*

The taxi took some inside roads leading into a village type of place. It was pretty cool. There were so many trees and little boutique-like shops. There were a lot of kids playing around, which was actually surprising 'cause the city wasn't all that far away. The car took another turn into a neighborhood and then finally stopped at a house.

"There you are."

The taxi driver walked around the car and opened the door. Lilly got out and paid the driver while I stared out the house. It was big and green. Like really green. Vines were growing from everywhere. I swear there must have been some growing out of the windows.

"Well, now we know that they have money." I glared at Lilly, who simply shrugged.

"And that they are eco-friendly, very eco-friendly" I did a hybrid of a nod and a shrug 'cause clearly it was true.

We began walking through the super healthy grass, my shoes making an incredibly annoying squeaky sound, which didn't help at all with setting the worried mood. Thinking back to the orphanage, this would totally be the kind of place, which we would ding dong with, and literally we were the first whose finger was pointed toward. There was a welcome autumn matt in front of the door, which was long overdue to take away, and a mixed leaf assortment reef hanging, which gave it a Martha Stewart pop of color to the dark door. I apprehensively took the fancy golden knocker and gave it a good two knocks as hard as I could, which at this point was as light as a cloud.

No one answered.

"Well, no one's home s—"

"May I help you?"

A woman's voice, just what I needed. Lilly stopped me dead in my tracks. I turned around, an older woman. She had blonde hair and soft brown eyes. Looking nothing like me, and I had no clue who she was, but apparently I was in her recognition list. Her eyes widened for a split second then went back to normal eye standard.

"Um, I just—" Get it goddamn together, Ash. "I need to talk to you and whoever else is in this house. It's kind of urgent."

"Sure, please come on in."

The house had a warm and cozy feeling to it with the distinctive smell of apple pie and coffee. These are old people, probably spending their time baking. She motioned for all three of us to sit on a couch, which had the typical flower print and crochet mats on the sides. Definitely Martha Stewart. She planted herself on the love seat across us.

"Hold on, let me call my husband." She turned to face the opening leading to the more interior part of the house. "Andy, come in here!"

"Nancy, I am watching the game!" A rough male bellow was thrown back.

"Andy, we have on demand, record it! We have guests."

A grumbling man walked in. He had a red polo shirt, short khakis, dark hair like mine, and blue eyes. Andy's face was wrinkled and looked drained out. Exhausted. Like someone was putting an elephant on his back, leaving it there for years. Just in case if any clarification is needed, these people are definitely my grandparents. His face whitened like he had seen a ghost, and honestly at this point, I wanted to be invisible.

"Nancy."

"Sit." She patted the spot next to her.

He sat, ever so carefully as if I were going to nuke him.

"My name is Ash." I turned to Lilly and Jake who looked ready to save me from anything. "This is my friend, Lilly, and my boyfriend, Jake."

"My name is Eric, and this is my wife, Nancy." He motioned toward the seat next to him. "Just so I know, why are you all in my house?"

Nancy look bewildered next to him. But it made no difference to him. He was rude, and at this point, I didn't even know what I did wrong.

Andy got up walking to a vintage-looking cabinet slipping off a scrapbook that lay on the open space on the top.

"A lot of things happened. We lost contact after a while. We were all done with putting up with the shit she made us all go through." He handed me the scrapbook in a not so nice way.

He reminded me of a snapping turtle. Wrinkly and brutal.

"Look, all we are trying to do here . . ." Jake was utterly undyingly pissed.

"It is the honest truth, kid. I don't sugarcoat this." He sat back, done, and cleared his throat.

I looked closer in his eyes. They were so blue, cold, and vacant, so icy and alluring. The funny part was that those same exact eyes were on my face.

"The only thing that will be sugarcoated is that you lack mannerism toward your own family!" Jake was on his face, fists balled, and eyebrows drawn in.

Andy got up abruptly. I could feel the anger pumping in his veins. The same exact genes which were interlocked in my DNA. I don't understand, why was this man so rude? I don't even know what I did. Lemme answer that, breathing.

"No, he's right. It was a waste to come here. It's not like anyone is going to be like 'Hi, hello, and oh, by the way, sorry we abandoned you without a single word for seventeen years.'"

I was raging. Literally I didn't want to deal with this man's hormones. He looked like he was going to say something but fumed out of the room leaving Jake at a distracted state and me with the last word.

"That went well." Lilly began to pick around her nails.

I snorted. That was an extreme understatement. Nancy sat where she was, staring at the photo album which was placed atop the table. The corner of the left side of her mouth rose ever so slightly. Then she looked at her hands, which were playing with each other.

"Follow me." She popped up and began walking up the shiny wooden steps.

It led into a long hallway with a couple of rooms. One was a bright yellow room, and the other was a master's bedroom. And it was huge. She walked to a jewelry box, the size of a treasure chest with a lock on it.

"You see, Andy stopped talking to Amber, but as a mother, I"—she pulled out some keys and picked the lock—"as a mother, I just could not not talk to her. I tried finding her, asked everyone she knew about her whereabouts. Then one night, I got a call from an unknown caller, and it was her. She said it was okay and not to tell anyone about her, that apparently she left for the better. But I guess that wasn't enough for me, so I talked to my son Jim, your uncle. He is a police officer, so he was able to track down the address."

She lifted up a shelf type of thing that was placed as a divider for two sections. She took out a folded piece of paper and looked down at it, hesitantly giving it to me.

"I . . . uh . . . I hope this helps."

I opened the note. There was an address scribbled on the paper in green ink.

"May I?" Her arms lifted up a little.

I sunk into the hug slowly. Her whole body shook.

"Dorothy, if those kids are still here, they better get out!"

Dorothy emerged from the hug turning around doing something I couldn't see.

"Come on." She sniffled. "You better get going."

She let us back down the stairs and right through the door.

"I hope you find her."

Then she slammed right on my face. Well, isn't that the best goodbye to the granddaughter you never had? I turned and began walking away. My whole life was composed of slamming doors in my face. Then again, this door was worth being slammed. I had an address in my hand and a somewhat smile on my face. Lilly was already at the car but Jake stopped me, putting his hands on my arms.

"Are you okay?" He bent down to look at my lowered eyes.

"Well," my voice cracked, dammit, "I am happy to have the address. I mean that's what we have been looking for, but then again I just, I guess I was looking for something else." I pushed the hair behind my ear.

He nodded giving me a hug, and we headed back to the taxi. The truth is, deep down, I guess I wanted to understand the feeling of being loved and accepted. Especially from someone who hasn't been there to provide it for most of my life.

*

I sat on the edge of the bed playing with my hair, having an epic stare down with the address paper. I was winning no, no I wasn't. I blinked at least twenty times.

"Are you just going sit there and stare at that piece of paper?"

I jumped at the voice of Jake. He was like a ninja or something, pop in and pop out.

"I was not staring!" I got up and began fiddling around with things in the room.

He snorted and came close, putting his arms on my waist and looking down at me. I felt like mush under his soft hazel eyes. Well, doesn't that sound cheesy? It does, so deal with it 'cause I was totally in love.

"So are you planning to do anything other than staring at something which isn't me?" His cocky grin never failed throughout what he said.

I smacked him on the shoulder.

"First off, ego check; secondly, I wasn't staring. I was taken with my thoughts." His eyebrow shot up.

"Yeah, you need some fresh air. I'm taking you out."

"Okay, well, I should probably take a shower. I probably smell funky." I got out of his arms, walking to the closet.

"Yeah, you do smell a bit ripe." I whipped around, sending a towel at him, which he caught embarrassingly easy. "What was that for?"

"You never ever comment on a girl's body order." A laugh bubbled its way up my throat until it burst from my mouth.

"Okay." Shifting his feet, Jake lifted the towel, taking the go-to-Shakespeare stance. "You smell as ripe as a newly fallen succulent fruit."

My eyes widened at the word *succulent*, and he laughed at me.

"Nope, don't ever say that in public or private, like ever." I took my clothes from the closet and began bum dashing toward the bathroom before he could see my flaming cheeks. "Go away, you flaming butt hole."

He blew a kiss to me, which made my cheeks hotter than magma, all Jake did was chuckle as he walked out the door closing behind him. Glad he had a laugh.

*

It was already night, which made me feel weird because we basically spend the whole day trying to make amends with a grumpy old man and then splitting a compromise with his submissive wife, who had a couple of lies behind her eyes. All in all, this twisted adventure was starting to swim its way out of this shit creek. Then again, it was exactly a warm welcome, so yeah, we were still sinking to the bottom of my personal finding-loving-roots mission. I dragged my Converse on the road as Jake and I walked, and yes, I still have absolutely no clue where we are going, and yes, it is annoying the hell out of me. Honestly, how many places could you even go to at night without overdressing, and I am not even overdressed, so if he is taking me to one of those fancy restaurants again, I'm probably going to get kicked out for my lack of style. I am totally scattered about this surprise.

"So mind telling me what this surprise is?" He sent me a side glance and a crooked smile. Yeah, I'm still so out of his league.

"Ha ha, nice try. I'm pretty sure telling you would beat the purpose of what a surprise is." He looked at me completely enveloping his hand in mine and gave it a swing, which could send me sprawling. "Then again, I think I would have to commend you for your effort."

I started to laugh hearing the distant sound of the waves. Was this sneaky little butt taking me to the beach? The only beaches that we had back at home were either too rocky to swim or the water was disgustingly murky. So either way, it wasn't pleasant. I know that Cali was mostly the origin for the best beaches, which is why ever single souvenir theme was either surfboards, surfer dudes with surfboards, or waves. And then the sound of music. Music? On the beach? At this hour? Is there some celebrity meet-up or whatever 'cause I barely know what are the recent movies that are playing.

"Okay, seriously, where are you taking me?" He slid me the same glance again, but his smile went up a whole feet, and as usual his ego was flaming.

"You'll see, it will take two more minutes." Now I felt annoyed 'cause he was talking to me like a freaking five-year-old.

"You're a butt," I said under my breath through gritted teeth.

His smiled bloomed once again.

"An awesome sauce butt." I rolled my eyes earning a wink.

Then at least two minutes later, which was so annoying 'cause he was exactly right, there was the distant view of a large Ferris wheel decked out with bright lights. So he was taking me to a carnival? On the beach? A beach carnival? I actually wasn't complaining whatsoever because I love carnivals. I remember when we were in first grade, we went on a field trip to local community colleges carnival. Rose and I had a blast. But when we went on the Ferris wheel, she peed her pants since she had the phobia of falling and cracking her skull open, and I won a small cheap dog with big blue eyes, which I adored. But on the way home, an actual dog got a hold of it, and yes, it was a tragic and scarring moment. I felt the feeling of total excitement pulsing everywhere, and a jolt of happiness electrified everything I saw.

"Hey." There was a blonde boy behind the counter. He was about our age, maybe a year older. "Entry form please."

Jake took out a folded piece of paper from his back pocket and handed it to the boy. He flipped back two strips of tickets and began to tie a bracelet onto Jake's wrist. Then I came forward, and he did the same.

"Well, you two have fun." The boy winked his blue eye at me.

The carnival was crowded with music blasting and the smell of deliciously unhealthy food. Everything was set up on the sand with the view of the ocean in the back. There were about a couple of rows of stands, which had those games where you win candy or a cheap stuffed toy. Behind all of that was a large lit up Ferris wheel, which pulsed with the beat of the songs. A couple or teenagers passed by, happy and underrated by the rotating world.

"I bet you, I can beat you at the first stand." Jake gave me a sly eye.

"Well, let's see about that. I'll take you out on that bet." I went ahead of him adding a little sashay in my step, which earn me with both his brows up.

"I am still going to beat you." He smiled at me giving me the seriously look.

"Uh huh, there goes your ego talking away." I used the puppet-talking-hand motion thing for further emphasis.

We strolled to the first stand where I kept my cool, which consisted of me looking like I had something stuck in my behind. The stand was a *Despicable Me*-themed water shooter game. Well, there went my confidence. Meanwhile, Jake looked like he owned the place. He looked down and smiled at me. I returned it with a pinched look.

"So, kids, what prize will it be?" The manager, if that's even a thing, was an elderly man with glasses. He leaned against the counter.

My gaze went through the multiple shelves stacked with a neatly organized supply of prizes, which could make a six-year-old squeal. Everything else was pink, so I decided that I would be nice and pick the brown stallion. Just 'cause if I lose this game, Jake wouldn't have to walk around with a press-me-to-neigh pretty in pink pony. Yeah, don't think he would be game for that.

"Which do you want to gift me, Blue Eyes?" Oh, it was sooooo on.

"I want the brown stallion." I shot a smile, which was dripping with sweet ice. I learned a bit from "Grandpa."

"Okay." The man moved from behind the counter and toward the control panel. "Ready? Go!"

I need to have a strategy. Jake shot two minions and one just ducked on my side. Never mind, screw strategy. I began shooting at some of them, but the pressure of my water-gun thing was way too low. Ugh, stupid minion water-rigged game. Jake shot another two making his total five meanwhile I had one. At this point, sucking was a major understatement.

"How you doing over there, Blue Eyes? I can just see that stallion galloping into my arms." He made a gesture with his head keeping his eyes on the target and hands clutching the gun.

"Shut up." I growled back as I began shooting randomly, which did absolutely nothing.

All of a sudden, the game stopped, and a red siren went off at Jake's side, a way to show off that he won. The man behind the counter handed the stallion over to a beaming Jake.

"Come on, Blue Eyes." He held onto the stallion, which made me laugh because it looked weird with his usual manly attitude.

He handed the horse to me, smiling a warm smile.

"You do realize I was kidding. You can keep the horse." I said, giving him the toy, only to have it given back to me.

"What am I going to do with the horse anyway?" His warm brown eyes soften when he peered down at me. "Also for all we know, you won the toy."

I smiled looking at him. From whatever he told me about his parents, it was like they weren't even related. He is kind and sacrificial, even if it was about the stupid horse.

The rest of the carnival was fun. I won a small plush Dory toy, so I wasn't complaining. I held Dory as we began walking along the edge of the ocean. Waves came crashing with the smell of salty water. Jake didn't say anything, neither did I. We just walked in silence listening to the story that the waves were telling us.

*

Nothing will ever be the same from when they left me to now, present moment. That was one promise I would make to myself. No matter the outcome, I will hold myself up like how I did for the past seventeen years. I will not, and do not, crumple at the feet of anyone. Some things were meant to remain for a long time, this was the promise I had made when I was thirteen, the time when I finally understood that she was never going to come back for me.

I quickly assembled all my things, looking over the yearbook for the second time this morning. Jake told me to meet me in his room after getting ready during breakfast, so I made my way over the connecting door opening it. His back was facing away from the door as he stuffed things in his bag.

"Hey." Jake turned suddenly advancing toward me swallowing me up in a gigantic bear hug.

It felt like eternity just simply standing there in his arms. Honestly, I wouldn't mind that metaphor being a reality, a so very beautiful reality it would be.

"Look," his hand pulled the hair behind my ear, "there is so many possibilities, just so, so many. And possibilities come with, come with a price, it could be affordable or out of budget." The corner of his lips tugged into a sad yet to the point smile.

"I'm sorry." My hands began to rub themselves on my short as they began to get clammy.

"For what?" An eyebrow shot up.

"Dragging you into my mess of a life."

To my surprise, all he did was smile holding my hands in his.

"I would gladly be dragged in the mess of your life any day, Ash."

ON THE OTHER SIDE

*

My heart was beating at the speed of light as I got in the backseat of Lilly's rusty pickup truck. This is it, the moment that defines me. *American Idol* suddenly made its way in my already huddled mind. But hey, it wasn't *totally* off topic. The contestants were chasing their dreams, I was doing the same. Just a bit more literal. Jake got in the car, waving a hello to Lilly, who just mumbled something as she typed a status update on her phone. I never really understood what the point of them are, might as well just walk around with a giant megaphone and announce what you are doing at random times. See how many people care.

The car went into reverse as we started cruising down the road. I took out my phone, which had been dead and abandoned at the bottom of my suitcase for most the trip, and plugged some headphones in. I let the melody of *Last to Know* by Three Days Grace wash over me.

I dedicate this to you, Amber, because when you left, I was the last to know.

*

A little girl stood in front of me. Dark hair, blue eyes, tan skin wearing some cheap looking clothes. She was looking straight ahead at the blinding light, I held my hand out guarding my eyes.

"Mom?" Her pixie-like voice chimed.

A woman emerged walking ever so slowly, almost timing her paces as if she were walking on clouds.

"Yes, my love?"

"Why did you leave me?"

"It was bound to happen, but I promise never to let you go again."

The girl, so naive, took her hand as the mother began to lead her toward the light. But something just wasn't right. I tried to scream. Nothing escaped from my mouth except for a whisper of air. I tried to run, but my legs wouldn't move. I just stood there watching as the little girl was getting eaten by the darkness. She turned one last time before there was nothing left.

She wasn't just a little girl, she was me.

*

Everything kinda came into a sudden end when reality came crashing in.

"Ash." My arm felt numb as I began moving. "Ash, come on, you gotta wake up. We are here."

"We are here." Those three words registered into my mind. I forced my eyes to open as I fixed my sleep hair. The side of Lilly's mouth tugged upward in a small smile. I readjusted Betsy over my shoulder as I walked onto the nicely paved concrete road, just to be pulled into a bear hug by Jake.

"Remember what I told you in the room." His voice muffled in my hair.

All I could do was nod and eye the house. It was big and made out of brick. Just as I imagined. There were two cars parked in the driveway, both looked well maintained.

"Okay, lovebirds." Lilly took her busy self and stood in between us looking at me. "No matter how much I would love to see you talk to your mom, I think this is something that you should do on your own with Jake. So Imma sit this one out."

I got pulled into another hug. Now that I look back, this trip involved a lot of hugging. Lilly pulled back and looked at me once again.

"You could do this. I am not the only one who believes in you." She turned and began to walk toward to the car, then looked over her shoulder smiling. "Go get em, Ash."

Jake took my hand, which I was pretty thankful for due to me feeling like I was going to bum dash back into the car. No, *no* I am not going to be scared. I am *not* going to let someone else's decisions dictate *my* life. Not today, not tomorrow, or the day after. Angry tears prickled the corner of my eyes blurring my vision. I walk-ran to the door, Jake keeping up behind me. My finger hovered over the doorbell.

"Go get em, Ash."

It was a spur of a moment. I rang the bell, and a man, pretty tall, probably in his midthirties opened the door. He leaned against the door frame.

"May I help you, kids?"

Well, he wasn't as scary as he looked. Jake lightly patted my back as I could do nothing but stare at him.

"Uh . . . hi . . . I . . ." My cheeks were probably red with embarrassment as his eyebrows shot up. "Does a woman by the name Amber Rowe live here?"

Smooth, Ash, real smooth.

"Yes, she does. Come in please."

My heart dropped as in crashing into my ribs breaking each one in the process. He opened the door a bit wider, and we squished through. We were led into a living room kind of area.

"Y'all can take a seat on either of the couches, I'll be right back."

The room was pretty nice. There were a couple of paintings, which hung up high on the walls. The couches were leather and actually kind of slippery. Let's just hope I don't embarrass myself by sliding off one of these things. Not that I have already embarrassed myself enough. There was some whispering coming from the doorway and then slow footsteps to where we were. Jake squeezed my hand, which made me look at him.

"You'll do fine, Blue Eyes," he whispered.

There was a small clearing of throat back at the doorway. That's when I turned around. It was Amber in the flesh. Her eyes which mirrored mine, widened, and she gripped at the wall next to her for support. We just stared at each other for minutes. I didn't know what to make of this. One part of me was angry *everything* in her house had its place, except for me, angry because of all the things she wasn't there to witness. But the other part just ached for her to show me motherly compassion. The angry part of me won.

Amber turned her head and began to walk toward the couch across from us and hesitantly sat.

"Small world, isn't it?" she finally spoke.

"You have no idea." My voice came short clipped and punctuated.

She looked down at her hands, which played with each other. At this point, her body language wasn't a midthirty-year-old woman but like a small child who was getting into trouble. I guess I was going to be the one who had to talk. *Don't worry, Amber. I am used to it.*

"You may be wondering who I am." She flinched at that. "I am Ashley Kaiden Rowe, your . . . daughter. This is Jake, my boyfriend."

Jake nodded a hello. He didn't even crack a smile.

"You also may be wondering how I was able to find our way to your house since you removed all information about you away from my documents." I opened Betsy and took out the birth certificate, placing it on the coffee table in front of us. "The birth certificate has an insurance code. We were able to track it down to a house. The house belonged to you and Lydia back in the day." Her eyes widened again. "From Lydia's house, I found this." I took out the yearbook, placing it next to the certificate. "We went to your high school, where we went through your records and found an emergency contact list. In that list we found an address to your parents' place. My grandparents." I took out the address which Ms. Romebotham had copied for us. "Then we went to your parents' place. Grandpa wasn't the most welcoming person in the world. Grandma gave me an address to your house." I took out the address. "This led us here."

The coffee table was lined up with papers when I was done. Amber eyed each one slowly stopping at the yearbook. She picked it up and opened to the page which I had tagged.

"So I am guessing you want answers." I nodded as she swallowed rubbing the heels of her palms across her face. "My parents were very egotistical. They always cared about their connection in society and they brought that down to me. It was like we had a zero-slip-up policy in our house."

I remembered looking through their albums noticing that most their pictures took place in galas or large events.

"My best friend was Lydia. She was the one person who *wasn't* driven by society, which made me like her more. We did art together in high school."

The man who greeted us at the doorway walked in with a tray of snacks and water. He smiled offering some to us. I took a glass of water and began to nibble on some chips.

"Some things were just not meant to last. My parents made me . . ." She put the glass to her lips taking a long sip of water staring at the yearbook. "My parents made me hang out with this guy, Austin Summers. They threatened me saying that they wouldn't let me go to college for arts if I didn't commit a tie with Austin. Our parents went to the same county clubs and became friends. When my parents found out about Austin attending my school, they had to hatch some sort of plan. They said that if Austin and I started dating, this could increase *my* popularity." She snickered. "But it was oh so evident that all they cared about was *their own* popularity. They had to be better than *everyone*."

Well. First, the first thing I learned is that my family is pretty messed up.

"Lydia stopped talking to me, and I never even knew why. Until I decided to approach her about it. She was really mad and didn't let me say my side of the story. I found out from her that my mother told her to stop talking to me. My own mother lied saying that she wasn't the only one who agreed with this, but in fact I had asked her to let her know on my behalf." Amber looked out of the window as if her life was written on stone. "I remember running home that day and just breaking down on the front step. This was never what I wanted, ever. So I opened the door and saw my mother seated at her usual chair, drinking a cup of tea, and I yelled. But she didn't even flinch, just shot me the I-am-only-doing-this-for-your-own-good look, but I knew better. I was just a toy for their popularity game."

I started to feel kind of bad, but I still didn't get the answer that I was looking for.

"Onward, Austin hosted a party. Like always, my parents forced me to go, so my mom got me all dolled up. I went to the party as someone I knew." She began to whimper and shake as tears rolled down her cheek. "And I left as someone I didn't. I fell in love with him, I fell in love with the fake him. The next time we got together, things happened. After a while, there were signs of pregnancy. Rumors began to fly. I went to Austin to let him know about it, and all he said was 'Do you think I am going to care for the thing?' He laughed in my face. After this happened, many families in the country clubs began to shame my parents. Their popularity went down. Soon after, my parents began to start blaming me for everything that happened. Look what you did, Amber, you destroyed us!"

She began to chuckle, but it came out as harsh sobs.

"Finally, one day, close to the date of your birth, they kicked me out of their house. Handing me some money and my insurance card, during senior year, Lydia and I bought a house in the woods that we would hang out in. We said that we would come and stay here while we went to college. That plan was long gone ever since my mother talked with her."

Amber got up from her place on the couch and took down a childish painting from the wall. It was just a small drawing, which seemed to be torn in half. She smiled looking down at it, then handed it to me.

"When Lydia and I were younger, we made this. One day, before I left, I went to my locker. It was the last few weeks before we were out of summer break. I found the other torn half of our drawing. This one that I have is Lydia. I turned the picture over to see that she had written me a note." Amber held out her hand and I gave her back the frame.

She took the backing to remove the paper inside of it, flipping it so that the words were shown. Apparently Lydia found out what was going on and offered any help she could give her.

"People would put so many things against me at the time that I . . . I just couldn't bear it. My parents kicked me out. It was the day I went into labor. I made my choice, I was going to start over. Leave all my mistakes behind. I had gotten an admission into a college, which was on the other side of California."

She looked at me swallowing.

"So I was a mistake?" I stood up. "I was a freaking mistake. I was never supposed to be there?"

My voice and breathing just accelerated after every word I said.

"Look I, I was not at the right state of mind. I felt sorry for myself. It was only for," she choked on the words, which were on the trail of leaving her mouth, "the best. I made sure that my name and information was blocked off from anything and everything. But I guess I knew that some way ends with tear, and you would find me. So I asked if they can send you into an orphanage located in New York. It was just far enough."

Angry tears rolled down my eyes.

"I attended the college and met Mason." She nodded toward the archway where he stood. "I told him about everything that had happened, he accepted me. We got married after graduation."

More tears blurred my vision rolling down my cheeks faster. All I was was a mistake, something that wasn't supposed to happen, something that was meant to stay broken from the start. My life was already chosen for me, and I didn't have a voice.

"I'm sor—"

"Save it. All I wanted, all I ever wanted," I choked out sobs, "was to be loved by my family, by my mother, and now I find out that I am nothing, nothing b-but a mistake."

Amber just sat there looking at me, sorrow in her eyes. Complete and utter crap.

"If you were ever sorry, you would have taken me out of the orphanage and be a mother to me. But no, make a wish, kids." I shoved everything in Betsy not bothering to wipe my face and began walking to the front door.

Nothing will ever be the same.

Sorry, but not in this case.

I was an unwanted bundle and always will be.

My hand jerked open the car door, which groaned in disagreement. Lilly sat as usual in the front tapping her fingers on the steering wheel with the beat of the song.

"So how did it go?"

I didn't say a word, just snuggled up against the window and watched as cars zoomed by. In the corner of my eyes, I saw Lilly turn to Jake, who just shook his head and put his finger on his lips. I guess telling her not to ask again. She nodded back, increasing the volume. I fell asleep to the sounds of the highway.

*

It was about six, and this was probably my seventh run since coming back. I felt kind of foolish, now looking back at how I wished my mother would be like. That when I would come to her, she would drop everything and give me a hug. Or do something motherly. Jake gave me a space. It felt bad not saying a word to him or Lilly for that matter. I made my way back into to the hotel when I felt that my legs were on the verge of failing on me. Pulling the suitcase, which lay right by my closet, I opened it up taking out my personal-relief-of-life-stresses notebook and dropped it on the desk. It hadn't been written in ever since my first date with Jake. Everything gushed out like a popped water balloon.

*

I ate breakfast alone attempting to pack up all my things. The departure flight was scheduled at seven. My tears had a mind of their own at this point, they flooded my face. Embarrassingly enough, it created a large damp spot on my shirt, which made it look like I was drooling, but I swear I wasn't. My fingers traced over the manila envelope holding my birth certificate.

Just one more look wouldn't hurt, now would it?

My name written in big light letters and the blank where my mother's and father's name should be. Cook's note fell out flying harmlessly to the ground. I bent down picking it up, sitting on the edge of the bed, looking it over one last time.

> Dear, Ash,
>
> You're doing something so very near and dear in your heart. Finding one person out of a thousand and putting the last pieces of your puzzles together is hard. But throughout your life, I have been there to help. The other piece of paper is a document, your birth certificate that may help through this journey. Remember, no matter what, everyone deserves a chance to live and learn from their mistakes.
>
> Love to you and Jake,
> Cook.

Maybe you're right, Cook. Everyone deserves a chance to live and learn from their mistakes.

*

I banged onto the connecting door.

"Jake! Jake! Open up please, I need to talk to you!"

"You okay there, Blue Eyes?" Jake opened the door, his usual hair was disheveled and his eyes were on the verge of closing.

I walked in, oh yeah, almost forgot to mention. He wasn't wearing a shirt. Yeah, it was kind of distracting. I motioned him to sit, which he did. Still without a shirt.

"Okay, so I have been doing a lot of thinking." I started.

"Oh dear," he muttered smiling. He put his elbow on his knee, resting his chin on his palm.

"Shut up." I smiled back. "Okay, listen. So I was packing, and I found Cook's note in the envelope, which held my birth certificate. I read it over, and she wrote a certain line, 'Remember, no matter what, everyone deserves a chance to live and learn from their mistakes.' After reading this . . ."

I stopped pacing around the room and looked down at the note, mentally re-reading it.

"I have decided that I want to talk to my mom. I may not be able to accept her apology, but it's either I talk to her now or never." I peeked up at Jake who was smiling with his white teeth and all. "But as the idiot I am, and always will be, when we went to go meet her, I was too pissed to get her contact information and all."

I sat down next to Jake fiddling around with note. He got up opening the drawer to the nightstand.

"Remember when we were at your mom's house, and I came out a couple of minutes later? Well, I told her that you need some time to think about things, so she gave me her contact informati—"

That was all I needed to hear. I jumped on him giving him a hug.

"Thank you. I think I'll talk to her when we get home," I whispered.

"No, thank *you* for finally opening up. By the way, Lilly is going to come before we leave."

I nodded into his shoulder smiling, closing my eyes.

*

There was a loud tap at the door. Jake and I were looking around the room, just in case we may have left something. I jumped over my suitcase opening the door, allowing the one and only Lilly to stroll in ever so casually. She turned her blonde head and pounced on me.

"I am going to miss you, Ash." I nodded back. She pulled back with a watery smile. "This has been some crazy two weeks."

Her hands rubbed my arms. She gave Jake a quick hug.

"You better let me know when you come back to Cali." She puckered up her lips in a threatening way, which only made her look like an idiot.

I began to laugh. "I wouldn't dare not to. You do the same if you ever come to New York."

"Hey, you never know! Future rock label producer might bring a band to record over there."

We all began to laugh, but it slowly died down. The truth is that I actually was going to miss Lilly. I think we both were.

"We should probably get going, Blue Eyes." Jake looked down at his phone's time. "The cab should be here any minute."

"Ash, make sure to call me when you get home. I'll walk you guys out."

We made our way down to the front outside of the hotel. I gave everything one last look and Lilly one last hug before Jake and I got in the cab and watched as the hotel became smaller and smaller. Until it was masked by palm trees and other cars.

*

There was a sudden pang in my heart as all the memories set it. The plane began to ascend into the clouds. I looked down at the landmass below us, my best and worst were made here.

Goodbye, California. I'll see you again.

*

I slipped on the ugly Christmas sweater that Jake and I had gotten from the mall a couple of days ago and sipped the steaming hot cocoa. We were both back in New York, where it was snowing like nobody's business. Today, it being Christmas and all, I decided I was going to call Amber.

"You look adorable!" Rose came over too.

I also had called Lilly introducing her with Rose and boy that was a sight. They were literally identical. We ran down the stairs like children to the sound of the doorbell. Jake came strolling in with a couple of boxes in his hands.

"Where should I put, these Blue Eyes?" He removed his gloves shaking out the water from his hair.

"Oh." I took his coat and hung it on the snowman hook by the door. "Just under the tree."

"So are you going to call her?" He slung his arm on my shoulder.

"Ye—"

"I hear kids."

Cook came running in stuffing a cookie in Jake's mouth, handing me the phone.

"You said you would call Amber when Jake comes. My eyesight isn't the best anymore, but I am pretty sure he is here." She pulled up a chair next to the tree.

I smiled at Jake, who ushered me to go on. The phone beeped as I dialed in the numbers.

"Hello." It was Amber, well, no shit.

I swallowed.

"Hey, Amber, uh . . . it's Ash."

"Hello, Ash, Merry Christmas." It was evident from the tone of her voice that she was smiling.

I took another deep breath. I could do this. I rehearsed talking to her in the mirror, which totally wasn't embarrassing or anything.

"Thank you, you too. Okay, uh, here it goes. I may not be able to accept your apology, but I don't want to forget about it either." I heard her inhale then exhale. Great, she was nervous too. "All I am saying is that can we start from where we left off. Maybe not as mother and daughter, but as friends."

It took a few minutes for her to answer, which got me even more nervous.

"I would like that, Ash. You are welcome to our house anytime you would like. I also want to pay for your college tuition."

Say what now?

"Uh, what?"

"I would like to pay for your college tuition. Sorry, hun, but I have to go. I think Mason just burnt the cookies. Be sure to call me later okay?"

I began to laugh and hung up the phone. I did it! Take that stupid self-caution.

"It's done. I did it. We did it!"

Cook chuckled. Rose did a weird happy dance thing.

"Okay"—Cook turned to the presents—"we should probably open these up before the other kids come."

I smiled in agreement.

"Ash, if you don't mind, I would like to give you a present from my side first."

Cook removed a flat object wrapped snugly in ornament packaging. I tore off the paper looking down a marble notebook. I had filled up my personal-relief-of-life-stresses notebook with the adventures in California during the plane ride back.

"Love," she goes, "I think it's time for you to start a new chapter in your life."

I smiled in agreement.

*

Epilogue

Twelve years later

"Good morning, New York, this is Laurene Masaquaninsikie, and today I am here with bestseller author Ash Kaiden Rowe."

The blonde most-liked radio host from the station Popping Hits 652 was right in front of me, and literally my mind was being blown. Like poof.

"Hi, Laurene. Hi, New York. Hi, world." I was really pushing hard to try to get the words out of my mouth before it cracked or an unexpected burp would leak out.

"So, Ash. You have recently published a book, and honestly it has blown up. One of the most-sold books, it's a memoir, mind telling those who haven't read it a little about it?"

I hesitantly chuckled.

"Um, yes, I have published a book, and it's a memoir of an important part of my life, and if you don't know, it's called *Chapter 1*. I believe you can get it anywhere at bookshelves as well as on Kindle."

Laurene smiled at me, and I am pretty sure that she could tell that I am as nervous as a person about to swim in a shark of tanks.

"And so there are a lot of people in it who are very important, so if you don't mind telling me what they are up to at the present moment?" She flipped her hair taking a sip of the steaming coffee.

I cleared my throat. Damn lumps.

"Well, who would you like me to start with?"

"Let's go in order if you don't mind."

"Oh no, absolutely. So Mr. Benson is still up and running. He has retired from the world of teaching, but he just couldn't stop his passion. So he opened up a small school, which works on the art of writing."

"How about sweet Cook? She seems very nice." Laurene's peppy voice was clearly intrigued.

I cleared my throat. Again.

"She is, I love her very much, uh, she still works in the orphanage doing her job but now she is the mother. The old headmaster who was there during my time sadly passed away about two years ago. So who's better than good old Cook to run that joint? And with that, she really put her loving touch, which I think all the kids in there need." "So sorry to hear about the death." Her voice suddenly became grave but then went back to normal. "How about Rose, your best friend."

I smiled at that.

"Rose actually attended Carnegie Melon University and studied engineering. She hated math in high school, which surprised us all, but tables turned. I love her, she's the best. And thank you, none of us even saw the headmaster very much. Mostly, if we got into some type of trouble. But it's life, twisted yet survivable."

"And Lilly, she reminded me of me actually when I was younger in junior year of high school."

"Lilly actually followed her dream and became an uprising rock band producer. She's pretty well known in that genre of music. She still lives in California, where she has an office, and yeah. We still keep in touch, she's unique." I began to laugh at that, remembering her feistiness, which resembled a fireball.

Laurene smiled, and I could most definitely tell what she was going to ask. Sneaky, sneaky host.

"So how about Jake, do I hear some wedding bells in the future?"

Yup, that was coming my way like a car at 200 miles per second. I look down at the diamond that was nestled on my ring finger, left hand, which refracted the light from each sharply crafted edge.

"Yes. Jake proposed last year right after I published my book, which was amazing. He's honestly the best, and I love him dearly.

He is into art recently having one of his amazing paintings in the national museum of art, so I am really happy for him."

"Aww so cute, congratulations. I have a bachelorette party to set up!" She smiled bright. "So you are twenty nine, I believe right, and how did you decide to actually publish this book?"

"Yes, I am twenty-nine turned older last month. In college, I attended Oxford. I was doing my degree in journalism, and I had an essay to do which had to be about important discoveries. If I recall, I was superduper bummed 'cause I had absolutely no clue what to do. So at night, I Skyped Jake since he went to NYU, and I asked him what I should do. So he said that try looking in your old stuff, you'll find inspiration somewhere. And literally I had a shoe box where I put important mementos in, and I found my personal-relief-of-life-stress notebook, which was the *Chapter 1* of my life. So I took basically whatever I wrote there and handed it in praying for an A, which I got, and my teacher wanted to talk to me after class. She was like, this was an amazing memoir, so she said I should publish it. At first, I was like pssh, yeah no. But then I reconsidered it, and then later after graduating, I published it. I thought it would do well and critiques would spit on it, but to my utter surprise, they like it. And I want to give a huge shout-out to all the people who loved and read the book, thank you so, so, so much, it means a ton!"

"Okay, thank you so much for coming to this radio interview on the station Popping Hits 652. This is Ash Kaiden Rowe, author of bestseller *Chapter 1* with Laurene Masaquaninsikie."

"Thank you so much for having me. Please buy the book today, and I hope you enjoy it!"

Well, that wasn't as bad as I thought it would be. Laurene clicked a button, and someone yelled we were off. She got off the chair and pulled her stylish sweater down jutting her hand out.

"It was a pleasure to meet you, Ash, and I loved your book, so amazing what you went through. Yet you accepted it." She shook my hand softly and smiled revealing super white and straight teeth.

"Well, mistake has the word *take* in it, and sometimes you have to take a chance by accepting and moving on, which is what I had to learn in *Chapter 1*."

We talked a little bit more until I said I had to go. Jake and I had a dinner with my mom, who came to visit to plan the wedding. A black car pulled up in front of the amazing building. I opened the door.

Life is too short. Take that sledgehammer and break the wall in front of you because in the other side, it is so much more than you could ever imagine. Trust me, I know.

CPSIA information can be obtained at www.ICGtesting.com
Printed in the USA
BVOW08s0716150516

448139BV00003B/201/P